FAMILY LOVE
AFFAIRS

Other novels by IMAFI

Family Affairs
Hold Your Judgment

FAMILY LOVE AFFAIRS

A NOVEL

Imafi

iUniverse LLC
Bloomington

FAMILY LOVE AFFAIRS

iUniverse books may be ordered through booksellers or by contacting:

iUniverse LLC
1663 Liberty Drive
Bloomington, IN 47403
www.iuniverse.com
1-800-Authors (1-800-288-4677)

ISBN: 978-1-4917-1344-0 (sc)
ISBN: 978-1-4917-1346-4 (hc)
ISBN: 978-1-4917-1345-7 (e)

Library of Congress Control Number: 2013920404

Printed in the United States of America.

iUniverse rev. date: 11/23/2013

DEDICATION

This novel is dedicated to the memory of Abiola Funmi
Adedokun Aloba. May your soul rest in perfect peace . . . My
love will forever be with you.

ACKNOWLEDGMENTS

I want to express my appreciation to my friends and associates who took the time to review and/or edit the manuscript. I'm indebted to them for their suggestions and contributions. I also appreciate the extent to which they sacrificed their reputation and the frustrations they endured. I cherish our healthy and heated discussions to tone down the vulgarity in the novel. In the end, however, I won the freedom of expression debate, because I was too stubborn to agree with their golden rules, according to the norm of society. I humbly thank a couple of them that prayed for my redemption—they will be happy to know that their prayers must be working, because I'm still breathing and untouched by Lucifer's tentacles, at the time I clicked 'save' to end the novel. Since I'm on a roll, let me also give glory to my God for His understanding and forgiveness. I'm certain, I will be back, to ask Him for more forgiveness, in the near future . . . definitely at the end of my next novel.

PRELUDE

*Glossary of main characters of Family
Affairs, published, June 2012*

Pastor Shackles

He is an African-American Senior Pastor of 5th Mount Olive
Baptist Church in Newport News, Virginia, who went to
Kumasi, Ghana, Africa, to find a wife. He met and married the
former Miss Kediri Yembe. They have three children: Samoa
(daughter), who was conceived in Kumasi and two sons born
in the United States of America. Pastor Shackles is rumored
to be more than just a spiritual leader and supporter of Dr.
Precious Riodiaz Dansford, his church's music director. He is,
however, beloved by his church and the community at large.
He frequently conducts humanitarian missions in Africa. He
has built five missionary primary schools in two West African
countries and five water wells in five villages in Togo and the
Republic of Benin.

Florence Shackles

Florence She is the wife of Senior Pastor Shackles. She changed
her first name, Kediri, to Florence when she converted from her
Islamic family religion to Baptist. Born in Kumasi, Ghana, West
Africa, she met, dated, and married Senior Pastor Shackles after
her fiancé was killed by a terrorist bomb in Kenya, East Africa.
She has three children with her husband: Samoa (daughter),

Nkrumah (son), and Martin (son). She is also the Assistant Pastor of her husband's Church. She is a member and co-chair emerita of her graduate school sorority, *XXX Bunny, Inc.* She has a master's degree in religious philosophy and currently pursuing her PhD on the birth and influences of foreign religion in developing countries—Ghana as case study.

Samoa Shackles

Samoa is the daughter of Florence and Senior Pastor Shackles. She is a lesbian who falls in love at an early age with Alice, the daughter of Dr. Precious Riodiaz Dansford. She is now living happily with Alice after family rejection of their lifestyle. She is currently a pre-law junior student at a university near Atlanta.

Michael Riodiaz

Michael was married to Precious Riodiaz, now Dr. Precious Riodiaz Dansford. They have a daughter, Alice. He divorced Precious, remarried, and is currently separated from his second wife. He supports his daughter's sexual orientation. After twelve-year absence from his ex-wife and daughter, Alice, he came back to attend her children's baptism during which he fell sick at the podium while delivering his fatherly-love speech. He temporarily lived with his ex-wife during his recuperation and attempted to rekindle his lost love with her. He had a son by a girlfriend before his marriage to Precious. He also has another son, Michael, with his current wife, attorney Lolita Riodiaz.

Precious Riodiaz Dansford

Precious was married to Mr. Michael Riodiaz and has a daughter, Alice. She divorced Riodiaz, reconnected, and rekindled her love with her high school sweet heart, Jeremy Warren. During their relationship, she had an affair she desperately wanted. She received her PhD online in socio-economic management in developing countries. She also has an eighteen month old baby girl, Moji, nineteen years after giving birth to her first daughter, Alice.

Alice Riodiaz

Alice is Mr. Riodiaz and Dr. Riodiaz Dansford's daughter. She is a lesbian and madly in love with Samoa, the daughter of Mrs. Florence and Senior Pastor Shackles since they were in grade school. Alice became pregnant after a series of sexual affairs including one with her chemistry professor, Dr. Ike Diick. She is now a sophomore pursuing early childhood development at a local university in the suburb of Atlanta.

Jeremy Warren

Jeremy is Dr. Precious Riodiaz Dansford's high school sweetheart. He reconnected with her after her divorce and his distinguished military service. He was on drugs for a period of time but kicked the habit He was loyal to Precious until he committed an unforgivable family sin and subsequently committed suicide.

Dr. Ike Diick

Diick is the chemistry/drama professor and Alice's chemistry 101 teacher. He was accused of raping Alice during their last dinner date.

Holy Father Jones

Father Jones is the Chaplin of the Main Street Hospital. He witnessed the taping and the reading of the last will and testament of Jeremy Warren before he committed suicide.

CHAPTER 1

Riodiaz had fully recovered at the home of his ex-wife, Precious. They custom built the house twenty years ago as a loving couple. It was a familiar environment he will forever wish he kept.

As a result of his ex-wife's hospitality and consideration, Riodiaz (Rio), was able to convince himself there might be another chance to rekindle the love he left behind (abandoned was more like it) twelve years ago.

He never forgot the intimate memories they once shared. He remembered the good times. He remembered their intoxicating laughs together. He remembered the sex they had everywhere imaginable in the house. He particularly remembered their first date at the café and the subsequent passionate sex five minutes thereafter in her apartment. Most especially, he remembered her first rule of engagement: "Rio, your lips, tongue, and dick are all mine now. This is not negotiable."

Rio was still in love with her after all these years. He would always be in love with her.

During the weeks that followed his temporary stay with her, he ordered two dozen yellow long stemmed roses to be delivered to her office every Monday and Wednesday, and one dozen short stemmed red roses for each of the other days of the week, except Saturdays and Sundays. On these days, the flowers were two-dozen white roses in an Italian vase delivered to her house where he was currently a guest and recuperating—his former place of residence during their eight-year marriage. He wanted his old life, wife, and familiar environment back, if only God would answer his prayers. Sadly for him, it seems his personal file hadn't reached the Lord's desk for consideration, if it will ever be.

Each card accompanying the roses was signed with the same notation, "To my love and soul mate, Precious. Please, forgive me. I never stopped loving you."

However, she respectfully turned down his every move and gestures. "We have been divorced for over twelve years and I've moved on. Rio, you may be my first real love, but I have found another man," she told him emphatically. She was at peace with herself and the new man in her life.

Several times, while recuperating, he had seen her breasts perkier than ever while breast-feeding her eighteen-month old daughter, Moji, in the sunroom.

For a thirty-something-year old lady who had breast fed her first daughter Alice, nineteen years ago and now nursing a newborn, her breasts were full, perfect, and more desirable to him than ever before.

She had equally seen Rio eyeing her breasts a few times. She always smiled, turned away, covered herself, and commented, "Rio, watch your eyes. You had lost your claims on these succulent melons. Moji and her father have won the right to suck them exclusively."

She was also flattered but uncomfortable by his flowers, unwelcomed renewed attention, and romantic gestures. She had really moved on, and any chances that Riodiaz would ever sample her "Coochy coo" again were little to none.

On a warm spring day, Friday evening of March 30, 2012, to be exact, she tucked in her daughter for the night and walked back to her den. She was only wearing a plain sweat suit to avoid any sexual attention or attractions. With a glass of lemonade, she invited Riodiaz for a chat:

Rio, I want to speak with you uninterrupted. This isn't a two-way conversation.

I want to speak my mind as I see things. Please, listen to me carefully.

Things have changed between us. Things can't be the same.

You always knew how straight forward I was with you. I'm still like that.

I no longer have the same feelings for you that I did during our marriage.

I once loved you dearly but I've moved on. Life isn't perfect but I had accepted my destiny many years ago after you left us.

I don't want to sound mean, but your pussy (I mean, my pussy) now belongs to someone else.

Many nights after you left us, I hated you with the same passion that I once loved you. Remember our first date at the café and the subsequent encounters?

Many nights after you deserted us, I fingered myself to wetness with you in my thoughts. And yes, many nights I placed your face on another man's body just to reach orgasm. I don't have those thoughts or images of you any longer.

Henceforth, please, concentrate your love and efforts on your current family. I felt your unresolved love and pain for me in your messages at the church. You know exactly how I felt when you selfishly and prematurely abandoned us.

I'll confess that I've not found anyone exactly like you since you left. I'm also old enough to know that I may not find another you. But again, I can't have all I ever wanted in one man.

Life goes on. My life goes on. Your life must go on without me too. I've found a replacement. The new man in my life may not be perfect, he will do for now. You must agree that twelve years was a long time to betray me after I had identified, coached, trained, tamed, loved, and branded you to be my King Kong. Rio, I've found me a new King Kong.

I once told you that your lips and dick belonged to me forever but you left me and gave them to that bimbo without my permission. You violated your sacred oath to me, and for that, I am over you mentally and emotionally.

Our only connection, henceforth, is our daughter and her twin sons. That's how it will be. It would be better for both our sakes if you leave my house in a couple of days.

One more thing, Mr. Riodiaz . . . Although I appreciate the flowers, stop sending them. I've instructed my office to send them to the assisted living facility of Celebrate Long Life, Incorporated.

Before heading back to her room, Precious gave Riodiaz a kiss on his forehead for the first time since his arrival, and said aside, "I'm done with that stage of my life."

While still sitting all alone, Rio thought of how he had planned to profess and accelerate his everlasting love for Precious before her evening's farewell rejection speech. He had contemplated being on his knees once or twice since his arrival to ask her to marry him again, even though, he's still a married man.

He was determined more than ever, after overhearing her nightly heated argument on the phone with an unknown caller. Precious never mentioned his name during the telephone calls.

Now that he had left his current wife practically for good, he felt he could appeal to his ex to give him another chance. Yes, he found what he didn't like; he thought his old charm would convince her to reconsider his affection now that she is single with a baby. He was very wrong.

He correctly assumed the nightly telephone conversation must have been between her and her new lover—her new King Kong, she had just introduced in her one way speech.

His suspicion was confirmed by the stack of love letters he stumbled upon in her bedside drawers earlier in the week. Yes, he was nosing around.

He opened one of the unsigned American greeting cards from an unknown lover:

From the moment I saw you, I wanted to meet you.
From the moment I met you, I wanted to know you.
From the moment I knew you, I was in love with
you. From the moment I loved you, I wanted to share
my life with you . . . And from that moment to this

moment, and for all the moments to come, I will love you with all my heart.

Also, enclosed with the card, was a hand written note that continued to profess the secret admirer's undying love:

Dear Prie:

I am very glad to have met you today. Since you left the events, I wanted to be with you forever. You excite me. You gave me the opening to want to love again. Yes, I know we just saw from afar, it must be God in His infinite wisdom that made it possible. Today is the day I will never forget because you are the most beautiful lady in the world. I'm increasingly happy to have seen you. You may not realize it, I feel alive knowing someone like you exist in this crazy world. I feel at peace from within. You are peace on earth. Please, share that peace with me.

What's more, I want more and more of you each passing day. As for me, it was love at first sight. Although I may not be able to explain it adequately, I hope one day you will understand why I feel the way I feel about you.

In my opinion, I deserve you. I deserve all you have to offer. You're the best. I have no apology for deserving the best. I am aware of your current situation; I just ask that you keep an open mind. Please, give me a chance to open your heart with my key of love and let me dwell within the warm walls of it.

I'm not in a hurry. Take all the time you want. I'll be waiting for you at the end of our rainbow whenever you decide to give me my happiness you're holding hostage in your heart.

Enclosed is a portrait sketch of you the first time I laid eyes on you. I hope you'll get used to it because I'll sketch you each day from the thoughts of you.

When you give me the opportunity, I'll read you the songs of Solomon to show you a sample of my admiration for you.

Signed: With all my love. March 6.

While sifting through all the letters and cards in the bedside drawer, Riodiaz also noted one more thing—there was at least one American greeting card each day of the week from the unsigned admirer. He knew he wasn't in a position to be jealous, but he was.

Two days later, all correspondences and cards disappeared from the bedside drawer. He felt guilty and shameful for violating the privacy of his hostess/ex-wife. He knew for the final time that he had lost any chance to reconnect with his precious Precious.

What he couldn't comprehend was how Precious could accommodate or entertain a new lover so quickly after the death of her fiancé, Jeremy, the father of her new born daughter, Moji.

But Rio got his timeline wrong. With simple second grade arithmetic, he would've deduced that Jeremy was in a coma for ten months before his planned suicide eleven months ago. He ought to know better that Precious of all people, can't do without a hard rod pumping her pussy beyond twenty four hours—the most she had gone without sex was the medically required six weeks' reprieve after delivery.

Riodiaz's brain must have been on ice since he left twelve years ago to have forgotten the details about her sexual needs and romantic demands.

He ought to known this fact because he experienced it during the weeks following the birth of their daughter, Alice. Even then, she instructed him how to pleasure her in another marvelous and memorable ways.

Although Precious suspected the sender's identity of the unsigned letters and cards, she ignored the temptation to open her heart to the affair she seriously wanted but determined to ignore. From her gut feeling, she knew the secret admirer was her type, if only sexually—any other considerations would have to come later. If her suspicion was right, she had been at a crossroad the first time she laid eyes on him at a distance. She refused to accept it as love at first sight.

Her only problem at present was that history may be repeating itself. She started the same way with her ex, Riodiaz, based solely on good looks, bombshell sex, and the thought of a big dick to fulfill her sexual cravings.

Detached observers would probably think she was a control freak. There was nothing further from the truth. She was just a calculated love vixen who had to have it and when she has to have it. She was like a determined, hungry, and poisonous python that must have its prey. Like the python, she just wanted a dick when she wanted it.

To have one good dick, one at a time, was her watchword. Neither Riodiaz from her past nor the stranger of the present had a chance at her paradise, for now.

She knew the power of being a woman. Contrary to popular belief, she knew the good Lord made women the leaders of the world. "Women haven't realized the potency or gravity of their powers," she had counseled her friends and foes, many times.

In some African communities, women may not be kings but they choose the kings.

Women had caused wars among nations and cultivated peace at the same time, from time immemorial. In all cultures, many men haven't been able to do without women.

She could never comprehend why her female friends never choose their battles wisely. To her, it wasn't a matter of who won a fight but which fight was fought and won successfully. She won almost all her battles, one reaction at a time.

She knew her role as a woman. She knew her roles and responsibilities as a wife. As a single woman, she knows what she wanted. She also knew what her men needed or wanted. She wanted to be her own woman.

She had one philosophy—she never subscribed to compromises. According to her, what was right was right, regardless of who was the originator of the righteousness. She knew how to love and serve her men, the same way her men knew how to serve her joyfully.

She once told her daughter a Nigerian parable on patience and control. It went like this:

A married woman, Bimbola, had a traditional husband who went out every evening without any consideration for her. She never complained. Upon his return each night, she would welcome him home with open arms and asked how his evening went. She would dress well for him as a sweet wife before serving him his favorite dinner regardless of the time of night. After his dinner, she would clear the table and bid him good night as if all was well. If she had any pains, she never let it be known to her husband.

Her only solace was her daily readings before bed, Psalm 37:7-9:

Be still in the presence of the Lord, and wait patiently for Him to act. Don't worry about evil people who prosper or fret about their wicked schemes. Stop being angry! Turn from your rage! Do not lose your temper, it only leads to harm. For, the wicked will be destroyed, but those who trust in the Lord will possess the land.

Bimbola continued her tempered reactions to her husband's extracurricular activities and neglect until one day her husband came back home earlier than usual, and asked his wife, "Bimbola, why are you doing this to me? Every day I went out, you never questioned me. You served me my dinner and never nagged. Bola, I don't understand your intentions. So tell me, why are you overwhelming me with love and affection?"

Bola softly replied, "My husband, I'm your wife and I am doing all I can to please you and hold on to my family."

In short, that was the last night her husband went out alone.

Bimbola had won her war without a single bullet.

Precious then concluded, "Alice, this is the story about understanding. This is the story about patience. This is the story of choosing your battles wisely. This is the story of the power of women and how that power was used effectively."

.

CHAPTER 2

Riodiaz had tried to move on. After his divorce from Precious, he had married Lolita, the daughter of a family friend he met at a family reunion. She was a brilliant lawyer, born to immigrant Brazilian parents from Rio de Janeiro.

He believed, marrying from his country of birth, might be more accommodating, rewarding, peaceful, and normal. He used to believe true love is culture and race blind. Once again, he was wrong.

Riodiaz's marriage to Lolita fell apart less than two years into their marriage, when they both discovered they had little in common. Lolita had stayed in the marriage mainly for her religious persuasion (she was raised a Catholic). His perception of Lolita's sexual liberation was naught, to say the least. He wanted another Precious or someone like her. To-date, he had come up short. He now admitted that abandoning his ex was absolutely premature, shortsighted, and stupid. He wanted Precious as much as he wanted to stay away from his current wife.

Precious's sexual commands and demands were his fetishes. Her life style was his desires. Her power over him was the power he cherished, wanted, and loved. Riodiaz must have forgotten that God, in His infinite wisdom, doesn't create two people alike. Precious was one of a kind. One fact was undisputable—Lolita could never be Precious. Finally, he concluded that he might be miserable for the rest of his life.

Lolita's breasts, although robust, soft, and inviting, never aroused him on the same scale as Precious' succulent breasts and hard nipples which, to him, were forever real and fantastic.

He had considered paying for the best plastic surgeon in the business for Lolita's breasts augmentation, if she wanted, so as to look and feel like Precious' 36D. But he knew the result would never be the same, *as the* famous classic song by Marvin Gaye, *There is nothing like the real thing* . . .

Riodiaz's wife, Lolita, was a workaholic doing her best to be the best female lawyer in her profession. After law school, she had devoted her life to her career and promised herself to become a partner in any law firm she worked for. She wanted to become a prosecutor within seven years after law school, a private defense attorney in two years after that, and a judge in five years thereafter.

Riodiaz wanted Lolita to spend more time at home. He pleaded with her for more nasty and exciting love making. He wasn't looking forward to the usual missionary position she wanted or offered anymore.

On one particular night, on their first wedding anniversary, Rio had called aloud Precious' name when he was about to ejaculate while making love to his dear wife, Lolita.

Even though he apologized thereafter, she pushed him away and simply said, "Take your stinking dick, and fuck the bitch then." Lolita never bargained for or conceived that their short marriage would end so badly, and so quickly. Sex, every fortnight, was far from exciting. It seemed Lolita's beauty and intelligence alone couldn't generate the passion of love she wanted from him. "What wouldn't be, will never be," she concluded.

Lolita was devoted to her marriage. She resisted any extra marital friendly dating or affairs. She knew her husband was not chasing tight skirts, except the one in his mind about his ex. It was the passion between them that had evaporated. "What a waste. What a pity," she silently said many nights.

After that episode, the love between them became more infrequent, stale, and boring. The love was gone by any loose definition or justification. Lolita tried to manage and rekindle whatever affection was left between them; but the thrill was gone from both sides.

Rio wasn't by any means cheating on his wife; he was just ejaculating consistently by stroking himself with erotic thoughts of his ex-wife, the unforgivable Precious.

Weeks later, Lolita filed for separation under the usual irreconcilable differences. In reality, they never had anything in common to reconcile.

They agreed to live separately and apart within the same household for the sake of their three-year old son, Mickey. She stopped using the kitchen just to avoid running into Rio. Two days after the separation agreement, she purchased for her room, a portable microwave, a portable refrigerator, and one of those, "As seen on TV" plug-in hot plate. Lolita is always flexible and adaptable . . .

CHAPTER 3

For over eight months, Lolita had been the lead counsel of her law firm in an initial public offering (IPO) for a .com company headquartered in the Valley. She had worked closely with the company's CEO and Vice President of Finance, Frank Gilbert, who also happened to be the grandson of its founder. Frank had a marketing degree from an overpopulated public university in Pichmond. Lolita attended many long meetings with him across the country during capital funding presentations to investment bankers and venture capitalists—it was rumored Pain Capital was one of them.

They both knew they admired each other, not for sexual encounters, but for their intellectual capabilities and similar tastes of the arts and Monday night football. They'd teased each other, on a limited basis, about their likes and dislikes.

"How is married life?" Frank once asked.

"Great. I am blessed. You should try it" Lolita responded with her signature sexy smile.

"How happy can your marriage be, when we've spent countless hours together for the past twenty three days"? Frank responded. He then immediately apologized for the overreaching and the inappropriate question and comments.

She accepted his apology. She knew he was right.

Somehow, Frank knew it wasn't his place or time to tease Lolita about her private life. He knew she was unhappy. At the same time, he wanted to tread gently for the opportunity to share in her strength, composure, beauty, and brain.

She had declined two invitations from him. One invitation was to a Broadway show to see whatever maybe playing. The other invitation was to accompanying him to The Louvre in Paris, in his corporate Beech aircraft. He knew it was a long shot that she would accept these invitations. Nonetheless, he was willing to cast his net as wide as he could to show her his interest.

Any red blooded man would have offered her the same and more in order to get to know and be closer to her. Any rational person or any irrational person, for that matter, would have concluded that Riodiaz must have been brain damaged to have let her go.

She would have loved to accompany Frank Gilbert anywhere he wanted but she declined gently, recognizing that she is still married. What's more, it would be a conflict of interest to date a client to whom she is the lead counsel for his corporate legal services.

As they sat in the conference room, she gently said, Mr. Gilbert, "It wouldn't be professional to accept your invitation."

Seconds later, she stood up, bade him good day, and walked away nonchalantly.

Lolita didn't want him to see her joyful tears of hope, happiness, and her desire to be touched and caressed by him. She knew he was right about her unhappy marriage no matter how inappropriate his words were. Deep down, she wanted to know him too. She wanted to share her hopes and happiness with him.

She wanted him but blamed the timing and her circumstances. She forgot, however, that everything in life has its time.

Frank had wanted her since the evening he kissed her hands and offered to take her to dinner anywhere of her choice . . . "My invitation is open ended, any time, any place, anywhere" he told her. He may be timid or inexperienced in women's sexual connections; he had great pick-up lines, for a young southern Caucasian man with a solid religious upbringing.

Although he was five years younger, Lolita loved the way he looked into her eyes each time they met. She was infatuated by the amount of attention he gave her. She was again bubbling like the beauty queen she once was during the homecoming parade in her freshman's year in college.

Most astonishing was how Frank had taken the extra steps to know her past, her present, her likes, and dislikes. He once had a personal note delivered to her aboard an airline on her way to Rome one day in summer. Lolita was equally surprised how he remembered her birthday with a personal video message streaming across her IPAD69 with her favorite lilies at the background. She was also smitten by the personal notations he always left on each page of legal documents he drafted for her review many times.

Lolita never wanted a divorce. It had never happened in her family history. She was determined not to be the first. She wanted to hold on to her marriage and convince herself that lasting marriage could be achieved at any costs, even in the face of loneliness and empty love. She wanted to do all it takes to keep her marriage for the sake of her son, conscience, and family considerations.

"Maybe when my son turns eighteen and goes away to college, I'll start a new life," she constantly told herself. Like all the women in Riodiaz's life, she loved him desperately for all the wrong reasons—I'll hold on to him and pray for God's guidance . . .

During one Sunday dinner, she spoke to her husband about the sad state of their marriage. She expressed her love for him, and how she would do everything possible to make their marriage work. Then, Lolita confessed to him how one of her clients, Mr. Frank Gilbert, had approached and flirted with her during their working sessions. She further told him how she turned him down and told him in no uncertain terms, "I'm still in love with my husband."

They used to tell each other everything. So far, Lolita seemed to be the only one doing all the telling.

She went on to say that, in order to avoid any temptations and conflict of interest, she had decided to resign her employment to avoid him, and also maintain her professional dignity.

"What are you going to do after you quit your job?" Riodiaz asked.

"My love, I'll open my own private practice and make do. Let's put the separation process on hold for a few months and see what develops. If we have to attend counseling, please love, let's do it because when I married you, I did it for love and for life," she told him as she held his hand with tears.

"Lolita, we shall talk about it when I return from the baptism of my grandchildren," was his short and abrasive response.

A day later, he traveled to OldPort to see his daughter and her children for the first time in twelve years.

Five days later, Riodiaz called Lolita to inform her that he had fallen ill and was recuperating at his ex-wife's house for a day or two after which he would be returning home.

"Please, get well and come home, love. We missed you love," Lolita responded. She repeated the word love one more time so that Riodiaz could remember her love for him while recovering at his ex-wife's home.

However, she couldn't recollect Riodiaz responding to her love salutations. She immediately felt the void in her life. All of a sudden, she was saddened. For a brief moment, she felt deeply alone. Lolita had had enough. She finally accepted that the love she so much cherished and wanted with her husband had become a statistic.

That night, she couldn't find any more tears to shed. She went to her son's room, kissed him lovingly and whispered into his ears, "My love, we are alone now. Your love is all I'll ever need."

She immediately changed into something comfortable and called her fill-in baby sitter to stay with her son for the night. Minutes later, she dialed Frank's cell and asked him to pick her up in fifteen minutes.

"Are you alright?" Frank asked. Her response was as defiant as ever, "Pick me up in fifteen minutes or if you're too busy, just say so." She was unhappy from within and unknowingly drawing Frank into the mist.

Frank's limousine was at her door steps in less than twenty minutes and forty two seconds.

Frank in his expensive silk pajamas was praying not to be stopped for speeding on his way to Lolita's. The drive time from his penthouse on the beach to Lolita's was over thirty five minutes, when going the legal speed limit.

"Take me to your house. I want to spend the night there" she said. He slowly eased the car through the Atlantic Avenue to take in the night cool breeze from the ocean.

Upon arrival, he showed her his opulent house that was fit for a king in a small kingdom, without mineral resources, in east Africa.

As soon as she stepped into his foyer, he offered her a glass of 1978 vintage wine (the year of her birth).

She looked directly into his eyes and said, "I'll give it to you, Frank, you sure know me well. I'm grateful for all your attention. Please, do not get me wrong . . . I want you more than ever tonight but I'm still a married woman and we can't make love until I'm officially divorced. I hope you can wait for me. I really hope you can. I need to take things slow for now."

As they sat on the couch, she rested on his lap and closed her eyes. At that moment, she was at peace and almost happy . . . Within minutes, she could feel his dick throbbing and poking her cervical spine.

As it turned out, Lolita was not sexually rigid; she had just not been discovered at the right time, by the right man, under the right atmosphere, and companion.

The adage, "A flower cannot blossom without sunshine or a garden without love," must have been written just for her.

"Lita, I've waited this long and I can wait even longer. I admired your openness and honesty. Just promise me you will never sleep with him again. Promise me," Frank reiterated.

"I promise. I promise," Lolita replied. For her, that was an easy promise to make considering the state of her marriage.

They went to the balcony and slept on the mat under the stars while they reminisced about their past and what the future might hold.

As they were drifting off to sleep, she couldn't believe her ears when Frank told her that he was still a virgin. Lolita immediately stood up, went into the guest bedroom, and locked the door. She felt guilty, inadequate, and almost unclean, as if she had just enticed an underage boy for illegal and dirty sex.

After a few seconds, Frank knocked at the guest bedroom and said, "Lolita, please open the door. Have I said something to offend you?"

"Please, Frank, just give me a minute alone. I'm sorry . . ."

Confused like a teenager with illicit and secret first love affairs with the young housemaid, she closed her eyes in joy because she knew she had found love in an unexpected man. With happiness from within, she thought about patience and recited Corinthians 13:4-8:

> *Love is patient, love is kind. It doesn't envy, it doesn't boast, it isn't proud. It isn't rude, it isn't self-seeking, it isn't easily angered, and it keeps no record of wrongs. Love doesn't delight in evil but rejoices with the truth. It always protects, always trusts, always hopes, and always perseveres. Love never fails.*

Lolita couldn't sleep. By 3:12 am, she tiptoed out of Frank's little castle, called a cab, and went home.

The next morning, she called her office assistant and asked him to transfer all Frank's company files to her firm's managing partner and promised to explain the details when she returns to the office the following day.

"Is everything ok?" her secretary asked.

"Yes, I'm. Thanks for asking. I just need some time to think alone without distractions from office work," she replied.

Frank called her cell over a thousand times, no answer. She didn't know if she could live up to Frank's expectations. She was unsure if she could ever live up to the love Frank was offering: fresh, sincere, unique, and peaceful. She was still afraid to abandon her marriage for the unknown.

Her marriage to Riodiaz had taken away all her confidence.

Three days later, Lolita was called into her managing partner's office to explain her decision to excuse herself from the .com engagement.

As she walked into the managing director's office, also waiting for her was Frank Gilbert.

"Counsel, what is going here?" the managing partner asked.

She waited in silence for nearly one minute and then turned to Frank, "Good morning Frank. Thanks for the other night."

"What's going on counselor?" The managing partner, John Rodusky, Esq. (a.k.a MP) asked her one more time.

Lolita sat down, crossed her legs, and gave MP her resignation letter. She then read from her prepared text, "MP, I'm in love with Frank. I'm still married. I'm the lead counsel of the debenture bond for his corporation. Gentleman, if both of you put two and two together, it's obvious there would be a conflict of interest in my continued association with the engagement."

"But you can excuse yourself from the assignment and not from the firm. Why the heck resignation? You are a valuable asset to this firm," MP interrupted.

"For my own sanity, it would be better not to cross paths with Frank at this moment in my life. I hope you will let me be and find another counsel in the firm who will be more objective to continue the engagement. I want to be released from this excellent firm immediately as well. I can't handle him right now. I'm not worthy of his love. Not now. Probably never . . ."

Frank interrupted and asked MP to give them a few moments so that he could speak with Lolita.

"Make it fast, Frank, please. We have a board meeting with the risk management team in five minutes."

As he walked away, the MP closed his door behind him, murmured to himself, "Women and their drama. And they want to be president of our great nation."

Of course, Rodusky was a registered member of the Publican Party and the general counsel, pro bono, for the local Tee Parti.

Frank went over to Lolita, knelt in front of her and said. "I loved you, Lolita, before I knew you. I loved you when I met you. As I told you three days ago, I'm ready to wait for you until you're ready. I realize you were shocked when I told you I'm a virgin. That part of my life is my choice. I admire you. I may be naïve, but I'm a good judge of character. When you decide to have me, I'll invest all my love in you. I know we can make music together. If you're willing to give up your career for me, I'm willing to give up my freedom for you. I want you to reconsider your resignation. Better yet, let me be the one to excuse myself from the engagement. I can always move to Kyoto, Japan, to our semi-conductor plant until you're ready for me. I've discussed the matter with my grandfather and the assignment committee this morning. I have their approval."

"Thank you Frank. I'm just confused and scared right now. I love you too Frank, I really do," she said.

With a smile, she said to Frank, "I'll be at your place this evening to make us dinner. I love you. You already know that, right? Oh, by the way, forget about moving to Japan unless you want to put me in your suitcase."

They kissed, hugged—it was the beginning of a new love affair.

On her way to Frank's home for dinner, she stopped by the grocery store and picked up the ingredients sufficient for two Imafi shrimp salads:

- *Boiled eggs (two per serving)*
- *Lettuce (mixed preferred)*
- *Baby spinach*
- *Strawberries*
- *Feta cheese*
- *Seedless red grapes*
- *Caesar's marinade and an original ranch dressing ·
  Carrots (sliced or cut to size)*
- *Cucumber*
- *Avocado*
- *Tomatoes*
- *Onions*
- *Pre-cooked tail-off jumbo shrimp*

She then stopped at a Chinese all-you-can-eat joint, and picked up two boxes of Chinese food: beef and shrimp fried rice with broccoli, mushrooms, and green beans.

She served dinner as promised. Frank gave her a dozen white roses and selected his best vintage wine from the cellar to consummate their first dinner date. He complimented her beauty and the best Imafi shrimp salad.

The salad pleased his pallet so much so that he had no desire to finish his Chinese food. They ate in silence, in peace, and with love. His time has come. Her prayers had been answered.

They held hands for a while. For the first time, they kissed tenderly.

He turned on a soft music, the Barry White genre. They gave each other maximum attention.

She handed him an envelope, instructing him to open it after she had left for the evening.

For the first time in her life, she wanted to be responsible for her future. She wanted to delve into the future with her eyes open and her faculty intact and healthy. To her, love was no longer a mirage. She vowed never to repeat the mistakes of her past with anyone in general and men in particular. This time around, she wanted to be in love according to her own gospel. She may not have to wait long.

They sat on the love seat and kissed with passion. They shared true love with sincere emotions. It was the first for both. They knew they were meant for each other. They wanted the moment to last forever.

He wanted to caress her. He wanted to palm her perfect breasts. He wanted to ask her to stand, face him, and sit on his lap, so that he could kiss her and suck her hard nipples at the same time. He wanted to convince himself, maybe it was time to break his promise: "The wait until she was ready" part. He imagined how he would feel for the first time to penetrate a woman's swollen vagina. His promised land is fast approaching on the horizon.

He wondered how his first love encounter would feel. He wanted to experiment, live, all he had read or seen on TV about love making. He wanted her to know, although a virgin, that he was the best for her with a lot to offer. Love offering, that is.

He then asked her again, "Lita, can I kiss you?" They kissed slowly and long. They held each other close and tight as they kissed and caressed one another. As if she wanted to go all the way, she unbuttoned his shirt and started to caress his chest and nipples while they continued the kissing and fondling. Poor Frankie, virginity had its downside: he ejaculated within minutes.

She felt his steaming and heavy breathing during his happy moment. She never thought he would ejaculate that fast. Nonetheless, she continued to kiss him to avoid any embarrassment.

Frank stood, apologized profusely and went straight to the bathroom. He was in the bathroom for over twenty minutes, still apologizing through the bathroom door. He was really embarrassed. The never wanted to be portrayed as a "Minute man."

To protect all concerned from temptations, Lolita left in earnest while Frank was still in the bathroom.

In a note, she told him her reason for the abrupt departure. "I'll tell the truth and the truth only. If you're a virgin, then, I must be a virgin once again, by the time you have me. Forgive me that I have to leave, my love."

She ran to her car. She was now getting weak by the minute for him. She was questioning her ability to wait until the right time: to be a virgin again before she would have sex with him, flesh to flesh. For her, succumbing to sexual temptation was becoming attractive and rational.

On her way home, she noticed her panties were soaked with her juices. It had been a long time since she felt this way about a man. It has been a long time since the sight of a man made her shiver. It has been a long time she wanted to make love all night. It had been a long time she wanted to cuddle with a man, feel his dick deep inside her, all night long.

She was alive again, ready for love, ready to love, and ready to be loved. Frank was the man for her. She felt it . . . She really wanted him more than ever. She almost turned around and ran back to him and say, my love, I'm all yours, make love to me . . .

She was just not ready for another child, not when she is still married. She knows she will be pregnant if she engaged in sexual intercourse with him. She couldn't use any birth control due to her religious doctrines. She didn't want him to use a condom either since that was also not allowed by her faith. In fact, she would prefer the roughness and the force of a strong and long dick in her vagina. A condom would interfere with her sexual joyfulness.

She thought and considered the church approved rhythm method, but that was not a viable alternative since such method was recommended only for married couples in the event of inadequate family planning.

"Please, help me good Lord and do not forsake me now," was all she could say aloud as she pulled up in front of her house before parking her car. She went straight to the shower.

That night, she washed her panties immediately by herself instead of throwing them in the laundry bin. They were drenched with her juices. She felt guilty as if an intelligent government agency was recording her infidelity on behalf of her husband.

CHAPTER 4

Frank opened the envelope Lolita gave him and found a personality questionnaire contained therein with an attached note stating, "Frank, please, answer these questions as frankly (smile) as possible, at your convenience. Some items may not apply to you. I love you."

Matters of Concern

Health:

	Yes	No
Do you have any history of family illnesses?	☐	☐
Do you use Viagra or any sex enhanced drugs?	☐	☐
Do you have any mental illness?	☐	☐
Were you molested as a child?	☐	☐
Do you exercise regularly?	☐	☐
Do you want me to lose weight?	☐	☐
Do you have regular medical checkups?	☐	☐
Do you use illegal drugs?	☐	☐
Do you talk in your sleep?	☐	☐

Habit:

	Yes	No
Do you smoke?	☐	☐
Are you a social drinker?	☐	☐
Do you sleep late on weekends?	☐	☐
Do you listen to others?	☐	☐
Do you snort?	☐	☐
Do you sniffle?	☐	☐
Do you put back the top of a tooth paste after use?	☐	☐
Do you put away your things after use?	☐	☐
Do you like to eat at the dinner table?	☐	☐
Do you think you know it all?	☐	☐

Personality:

Do you like animals?	□	□
Do you like children?	□	□
Are you abusive?	□	□
Do you believe in 50/50 relationship? Explain.	□	□
Do you like quiet time for yourself? Explain.	□	□
Are you moody?	□	□
Do you like to compromise?	□	□
Do you like sports?	□	□
Do you think LeBron James should have stayed in Cleveland?	□	□

Character:

Do you respect yourself as well as others?	□	□
Have you been in jail or run afoul of the law?	□	□
Do you like a lot of jewelry on women?	□	□
Do you like mother-in-law?	□	□
Do you own a gun?	□	□
Do you like to flirt?	□	□
Do you attend church?	□	□
Do you have any secrets I should know about?	□	□

Romance:

Would you like to have children?	□	□
Do you like to make love in the morning before going to work?	□	□
Are you open to innovative sex ideas?	□	□
Do you like women to be and look natural?	□	□
Do you love watching porns in any form?	□	□
Would you want me to suck your dick?	□	□
Would you eat my pussy?	□	□
Can you make love at least twice a week?	□	□
Do you like wet kisses?	□	□

Do you like to cuddle? □ □
Do you like or envision nasty sex? □ □
Do you dream of having a threesome? □ □
Do you ever think of being with a man? □ □
Are you romantic? Explain. □ □
Do you believe in divorce? □ □

Finance:

Do you have a good credit? □ □
Do you have child support payments? □ □
Have you filed all your tax returns? □ □
Do you owe taxes to any tax authorities? □ □
Do you mind women making more money than you? □ □
Do you believe your children should go to private □ □
  school?
Do you have a will or trust? □ □
Would you prefer a prenuptial agreement? □ □

Politics:

Do you enjoy political discussions? □ □
Are you a democrat? □ □
Do you believe the so called one percent should pay □ □
  more taxes?
Do you believe comprehensive immigration law □ □
  should be passed?
Are you a Tee Parti sympathizer? □ □

Remarks
Add additional remark pages, if necessary.

_____

_____
_____
_____

Frank immediately answered the questionnaire with lengthy clarity and explanations where necessary, and sent it back to Lolita with a note, "Frankly (smile), hope I pass with an A."

CHAPTER 5

Precious called Pastor Shackles and left a message that she and her daughter would be staying at a local hotel until Riodiaz left her house.

Pastor Shackles had become her comfort and spiritual adviser. With a new baby and a dead fiancé, she needed Pastor Shackles to be her king Solomon.

He returned her call and welcomed the good news. Together they had a short prayer. "Thank you Lord," Pastor Shackles and Precious jointly said as they ended their conversation with prayer.

It seemed the power of prayer was working. Riodiaz left a day later. His departure ended the rumor that the devil might have tempted her to be fucking her former husband shamelessly shortly after the death of her fiancé, Jeremy.

She knew many admired and wanted her. Some of her friend's teenage sons even referred to her as M-I-L-F (Mother-I-like-to-fuck). She just didn't give a damn about what those under age seventeen-year old dysfunctional boys with raging hormones thought of and about her.

She knew she was addicted to any good, decent, and loving man with the ability to satisfy her sexual appetite. She was not different from any other woman of her tribe. And if her good Lord had endowed her with beauty, she was not about to feel guilty about it to anyone. With a flawless and smooth chocolate skin, soft body, and kissable lips, she has no regrets but grace to the Lord for His kindness.

To those who were jealous of her, she had one simple message: "Y'all hater-bitches can go and jump over the bridge that leads to nowhere."

Before her ex, Riodiaz, left OldPort, he had lunch with his daughter, Alice, her children, and her lover and partner, Samoa. They cried together, laughed a little, and prayed that they see one another very soon.

"Maybe, we will come for a visit soon daddy, and not wait another twelve years," Alice told her father. Alice had no clue of the tempest in her father's life.

He never told his daughter that his second marriage was coming to an end.

He did tell her one truth, however, "Your mother doesn't want me anymore."

"Sorry daddy, it has been a long time since you left us."

What an irony: Alice's love preference with her girlfriend, Samoa, not approved by anyone, was prospering, but the critics' acceptable brand of love, based on the norms of the society, were in shambles. "Physicians, heal thyself."

Surely enough, when Riodiaz returned home, his life was in a free fall and without the ability to stop it. Who he wanted, he could not have. Who he had, he did not want. That had been the story of his life to-date.

CHAPTER 6

Precious had met her anonymous admirer when she was estranged from her fiancé, Jeremy. They saw each other from afar one Saturday morning, on a raining day, on their way to a church revival during Lent. Although only one of them admitted it, it was love at first sight.

"I would love to reach an orgasm with him on a rainy day. Sweet Jesus," she told herself, when she first saw him from afar, on that raining day.

Rain was her perfect weather. The sound of rain drops against her window pane gave her goose bumps. She drove home wishing the man she admired would keep her company any raining days, with a glass of wine, chocolate covered desert, and soft music playing at a distance . . .

On raining days, with her bedroom lights dimmed just right, in front of her tall and wide windows, she would parade naked, her curved and tight killer of a figure. She had no window blinds by design. She never liked them. She never wanted them. She wanted to invite nature into her bedroom without any interference. She had always been a nature girl. She was once a carrying card member of the Audubon Society.

To her, those who have eyes to see all of her, holy Moses . . . let them see.

A thirty-something year old neighbor, Joyce, with four children, had seen her naked through her window a few times. All she did each time was looked briefly, turned away, and murmured demeaning words about a middle-aged woman behaving like teenagers. She forgot the circumstances surrounding the birth of her own four kids. Also, she is currently entertaining a 21-year old, named Stocky, every Thursday night. What an irony: the pot was calling the kettle black . . . Hypocrite

Stocky, Joyce's so called boyfriend lived in a housing project six miles away, next to a newly developed lower-middle class trailer park. Although unemployed, he volunteered as a little league coach to her son, Rodney. Stocky lived with his father, by default, after his mother went to jail for shoplifting a dozen donuts at a small sandwich shop on a Sabbath day.

Joyce's thirteen-year old red-head eldest son, Rodney, has an unavoidable habit of watching Precious' display from his yard behind tree leaves, on a daily basis too. Many nights, he had debated whether to do his homework or watch Precious live. Seven out of ten, watching her prevailed. Five out of the seven, he had lost valuable sleep during school days. His grades, already marginal, was becoming dismal as a result . . .

On several occasions, Rodney had seen his coach/friend leaving his house Thursday nights, hours after he had said good night to him and his siblings early in the evening. He had dreamt of Stocky driving home late nights on two occasions with his mother. He didn't want to accept that his coach/friend had been "Hitting home run" with his mother. He loves his coaching abilities. He loves baseball. Frankly, he didn't know what to do or how to react to his mother's cozy association with his coach/friend. He had asked himself many times, "What are they doing?" The poor little red head was clueless. Joyce was a cougar before the term became fashionable household word in the western hemisphere.

One late Saturday, Rodney, standing in the rain, soaking wet, with stolen binoculars, was caught watching Precious parading naked in her bedroom. Poor Rodney was sick with pneumonia for weeks thereafter. Joyce, who almost lost her son as a result, continued to blame Precious for her son's near death experience.

Rodney had stolen the binoculars underneath the driver's seat of a 1992 blue Ford pickup belonging to Stocky. Stocky also discovered his peeping engagement, one evening, and dragged his ass to his mama, Joyce.

Rodney had obviously inherited his father's genes. His mother had told him thereafter that he would be a pervert just like his father who was caught numerous times peeping into the girls' gym bathroom where he worked as an assistant coach at a private franchised technical college on the west coast, near the Mexican border. His father, who had since lost his job for that reason, was later sentenced to two-year probation and was registered as a sex offender.

So far, Rodney had proven his mother wrong. Or maybe, he had not been caught yet. After all, his father was caught of his sexual defiance at the age of forty five. If statistic is any guide, Rodney has time to catch up and be like his father.

Poor Rodney had seen and watched Stocky used the same binoculars a couple of times, inside his truck, while parked across the street from Precious bedroom for the same reason. At twenty one, Stocky was already a greedy and a perverted young man. It seemed, Joyce, was always attracted to the same perverted souls.

Precious had since stopped her recreational activities temporarily after an anonymous letter, taped to her front door, warning her to stop the free show at primetime. The letter simply read:

Dear fabulous neighbor on South View:

We all love all you do and how you do them. After a hard working day, you made our days better by your display. We particularly love you on late Wednesdays and Saturdays. But we just want you to know that our teenage boys may be watching too. Their school grades are suffering. Many have been wetting their beds lately. Please, slow it down a notch, at least, until late night after Conan's late night show . . . We can't speak for the minority among us with girlfriends or wives, some wives are complaining and threatening to call the cops or go to the city council unless you shut down the window shows. We don't see anything wrong with your act but please work with us and change your entertainment scheduling to late, late night . . .

We are your friendly neighbors and admirers.

The letter was unsigned.

CHAPTER 7

Precious wanted a new life with a new man but felt guilty leaving her live-in-fiancé of twelve years, Jeremy. Mostly, she just wanted to be happy sexually. Her new admirer seemed to have everything she wanted and more. She was now faced with two dilemmas—Jeremy, the real thing or the dream, hope, and fantasy she knew existed in the stranger.

Her admirer was different and exceptional by the ways he had communicated with her. She perceived the satisfaction and pleasures she would enjoy with him: he was pleasantly authoritative, assertive, and yet gentle. He was ruggedly good looking. She loved these attributes in a man, for a change. She saw and loved how he could challenge her. Education, wisdom, and humbleness had always been sexually intoxicating to her.

Her ex, Riodiaz, had attempted to meet her expectations during their seven-year marriage, the admirer was better by far from afar.

Precious never wanted to be the leader or head of her household, at least not all of the time. The men in her life to-date had been weak and compromising. She wanted a man she could look up to, unlike her father who allowed her mother to walk over him. She believed her secret admirer met her dreams and hopes.

She looked forward to the admirer's daily letters, sketches, and cards—he was understanding and forceful when necessary. He had promised that his heart belongs to her and said, "Jeremy is a good man but I am a better man." He had expressed repeatedly in many unsigned cards sent to her three times a week: Tuesdays, Thursdays and Saturdays, his emotional feelings. He hoped the United Postal Service will never cancel its Saturday delivery. "U.S Congress, please," he pleaded.

He had quoted in one of his letters a favorite African adage, "A fish and bird may fall in love but they can never build a house together," to remind her that he would be a better lover than her live-in fiancé, Jeremy.

"If you allow me, I'll take you places that neither of us has ever been," he had written her. Desperate and determined, he had included a faceless sketch of her riding his dick fast and furious while her tits dangled in his face. He sent it just to shock her into a response. Monet, eat your heart out.

She understood his messages as she viewed the latest sketch and said aloud, "He had not even met me, and yet, he has the guts to draw nasty shit about me." She smiled and kept the sketch underneath her panty drawer. Ironically, she loved his style.

For the first time, she loved a man who knew what he wanted and was unafraid to demand it. "Precious, what has become of thou," she asked herself. She really wanted to say," Shit, what the heck am I getting myself into?"

She wanted to connect with her admirer in body and soul. She wanted to know every inch of his body, especially every inch of his reproductive organ. She wanted to enjoy him if she ever submitted herself with desires to him sexually. She said many times, "Good Lord, help me in this time of my needs and temptations."

Her fiancé, Jeremy Warren, was now under full assault from different angles.

Jeremy was too late, however. A soccer ball penalty kick was approaching Precious' goal post at full speed, and Jeremy, the goalkeeper, couldn't stop it. The admirer was the determined penalty kicker.

She was not guilty of having an affair. Not yet, at least, even though she knew she was treading on dangerous grounds.

As her mind drifted, she recounted her encounters with her ex, Riodiaz, and their sexual escapades. Riodiaz was the first to discover that she enjoyed sex in different parts of the house for great and satisfying sex. She would like the same performances and more from the secret admirer.

She loved variety. Change of sex venues, she believed, heightened her sexual pleasure and satisfaction. The only way Riodiaz could remember the next place to make love to her was to name each room a different day of the week for a particular sex act. The bathroom was named Sunday because it was a day before the work week and plenty of rest was needed. Sunday's sexual encounters were limited to thirty five minutes maximum. They had their plans and it worked until . . . They even set the alarm on their iPhone to synchronize the length of time for sex.

Fucking on top of the washing machine during the rinse cycle was her favorite. That was on Saturdays. She had dragged Riodiaz to the laundry room just for the washing machine encounters and the doggy style she enjoyed. The vibration induced her orgasm within minutes. She was proud of her creativity. She smiled at the possibility of Maytag organization using this attribute in their advertising campaign. She knew that would never happen, however. Damn it . . .

She had a place in their house designated, "For pussy licking only" before the late light dinner: the balcony. That was on

Thursdays. She sometimes promised Riodiaz before the licking, "Your sweet creamy filled donut is ready before dinner." She just loved her desert consumed first.

Friday was set aside for fingering her pussy in their den or at the movies. No dick poking on Fridays, her day of rest.

Before this strategy, they'd tried leaving a mark at random in the house as some animal kingdom marked their territories, but that strategy never worked to their satisfaction.

They had had too many sexual encounters to keep track of the where, when, or how often. Even those with degrees in econometrics couldn't quantify their sex encounters.

She enjoyed the discussions after sex on any subject. She once told Rio, "Make me go to sleep after sex and you know you have satisfied me." Ever since, Riodiaz made sure he fucked her brains out. He always loved her sexual freedom and her ability to try anything once. They had no problems with sexual communications in their marriage. According to her diary, on page 356, they had tried many things more than once. The more they tried new ways, the better the sex part of their relationship gets.

But now, she wanted someone with more education, more exposure, more wisdom, more strength, and above all, someone with a longer and beefier dick to fulfill her desires—sexual desires. Although she might not live by sex alone, a perfect dick was her happy and perfect storm.

Pastor Shackles, his wife, Florence, and their church continued their missionary programs in Ghana and beyond. They'd strengthened their church outreach and expanded into such cities as Lagos, Nigeria and Entebbe, Uganda. They also established their missions into countries like Kenya, South Africa, Liberia, and Cameroon, as part of their 10-year "Saving Souls" crusade for Africa.

The African projects were the brain child of Mrs. Florence Shackles. She had doubled her efforts and forced her husband to accompany her anywhere she went, for the last two years when she was convinced her husband might be having too cozy a relationship with Ms. Precious Riodiaz.

She convinced her husband to accompanying her on every African mission as a way to hold on to her husband and keep him away from Precious tentacles and temptations. Her husband had denied any such relationships with Precious but she wouldn't believe him. No one would. No one did, not even his trustee board.

"Hang on to your husband," she continued to replay in her mind on the advice of her church gossip queens. Maybe, *Stand by your man*, by Tammy Wynette, would have been more appropriate.

Florence was human and made of flesh. She hated the thought of her husband sleeping with a beautiful and educated whore, Precious.

All her intensions weren't entirely to serve the Lord and His flocks on those African missions. She had been warned to "Watch out for the Hawk" by her unsolicited secret agents and friends. She knew Precious was the Hawk. Everyone told her so . . .

She had accepted that Precious' daughter, Alice, had taken her own daughter, Samoa, away for good, and now, she was coming after her husband. "That would never happen, except over her dead body," she vowed.

Florence had had so many visions, at least twice a week, of her husband's sinful ways. In one dream, she saw her husband at a distance, lusting after Lucifer (a.k.a Precious) and at the same time, praying to the angels along the trail to rescue him. She couldn't recollect how the dream ended. Her suspect of her husband's lust for Precious kept her up many nights.

If history were her guide, she knew the temptations in all God's children, especially among the agents of the Lord.

She had read all about the acts of church leaders. She knew the inequities of many TV evangelists and many who couldn't afford media blitz, about their rise to fame, their fall from grace, and their greedy appetite, and weakness for the flesh. She personally knew one or two of her church elders, sleeping around on their wives and a prominent wife in the church caught sleeping with the chairman of the single men's ministry at the cloak room.

Her husband could not have been better than those mighty men of God who had fallen in one form or another. To her, forgiveness was not enough when it came to her husband's infidelity. As far as she was concerned, she had given her husband the proverbial "One strike and you're out" ultimatum. She meant it too.

To show his love for his wife, prove his fidelity, and led by example, Pastor Shackles had always traveled with his wife to Africa to save the flocks, among other things.

What's more, their "African plan" was a lucrative endeavor for the church ministry as well.

Their African missions were unique because they went beyond the traditional church praying, preaching, singing, and giving testimonials to flocks that have not seen the light. They did more than handouts and preaching of the second comings, or the usual Sunday sermons that all believers will be welcomed into the Kingdom of Heaven, as long as they repent, pay their tithes, and ask for forgiveness . . .

The Church built schools and water wells for much needed clean water for villagers. It constructed rural medical clinics and funded small businesses for the impoverished housewives, single women, and farmers. They held their volunteers and church members of the host communities, responsible and accountable for their actions. Church members and volunteers were oriented not to participate in mental and structural corruption, which is disproportionably the number one psychological disease in Africa. The jury is still out in the management strategy and endeavors . . .

Florence knew there was corruption everywhere in the world, but the corruption in the continent of Africa was epidemic, disproportional, structural, and inhumane. She vowed to do something about it. So far, she wasn't winning on that front. She may never win,

On a good note, their church was well connected to local, state, and national politicians in every city and town they went. Such association and networking had allowed the church to acquire the natives' land at pre-slavery prices, all in the name of the Lord, their savior and redeemer. On several occasions, she told her friends, "Folk from China, India, Pakistan, Lebanon, and Germany, to name just a few, are taking over the continent anyway." Welcome to modern day colonization of a continent, this time, handed over by the countries' citizens, at a price.

Mrs. Florence's African families benefited too. Her parents had visited them in the United States. Her elder brother, Oko, had come to join them with a visiting visa.

Oko was the house sitter and babysitter for his two cousins while the Shackles were on tour of Africa and beyond. He had since enrolled at a local university and taken some courses online to pursue his first degree as a double major in economics and theology. He hoped one day to be "Just like his brother in-law", whom he referred to as "Brother Pastor Shackles."

After constant disagreements with his sister, Oko moved into his own apartment within three months of his arrival in the United States. He hardly spoke to his sister ever since.

Oko was born 38 years ago in Kurumbe, Gold Coast, the modern day Ghana. His parents hailed from the Yoruba land in Nigeria. He received his high school London matriculation diploma at the age of fifteen with concentration in social sciences. After his secondary school education, he worked for the Ministry of Finance for five years as an assistant to the assistant senior deputy (special projects) to the assistant Director of Sciences, in the ministry of technology, and cultural Affairs, Ghana. His cousin, Dr. Joshua Kutikuti, MBE, was the minister of the Ministry.

At the age of twenty one, he joined the armed forces for financial security and ability to meet girls of his choice. He was later posted to the Republic of Congo as military attaché to the Ghanaian's Ministry of External Affairs—African Union's peace keeping force division. In that capacity, he traveled to and lived briefly in many African countries and cities such as Zimbabwe, Republic of Benin, Togo, Congo Kinshasa, Entebbe, Chad, Monrovia, Enugu, Pretoria, and Mogadishu. He studied and loved the cultures and customs of every city and community in which he lived. He spoke six different languages fluently, including, Latin, English, and his native language, Kukusi.

As a former soccer star on the Ghanaian's national team, Oko was not a stranger to beautiful girls. Many of them were barely legal members of his fans across Kurumbe and beyond. Many were virgins. A few were his mother's age: single or the loosely married ones among them were willing to temporarily set aside their marriage wows in other to have a piece of him.

Every young and innocent girl wanted him. All mothers far and near dreamt of him being their son-in-law. Many girls of marriage age, and few old enough to be his older sister, wanted to have his children without commitment because they just wanted him, period. Some just wanted to fuck him and spit him out. Many among them, especially from his village, voiced their attraction every time they watched him play soccer on their town's free public movie screen, a gift from a church outfit in Texas, courtesy of the village King, Rev. Chukuma Toto.

He was a national hero in his own right. A super star recognized many times by the president of the country. His village King wanted to make him a Chief as soon as he is able to pay the required coronation and ordination fees. He promised to think about the offer because the asking price of twenty five million cedes was not a chump change. After all, he wasn't a member of the corrupt citizens. Not yet, at least.

One of his young and secret admirers, Eki, from the capital, confessed to her mother, "I don't care if he takes care of my baby; I just want to have his child." Eki was the daughter of a Senator and a former Commissioner of Justice of the federation, finance minister, and secretary of inland security. Her father had promised to arrange it. After all, he had appointed Oko's cousin, Dr. Kutikuti to his current ministerial position.

Eki was considered in her secondary school as the most beautiful girl in a decade. She was voted to be the only one expected to marry a politician or a soccer star before the age of nineteen.

Everyone in her school called her, a rich bitch.

Before graduation and before her father could arrange her encounter with Oko, her loose life style caught up with her and became pregnant. Her father later shipped her to England in the dark of night to cover up the family's shame. There, she had an abortion, courtesy of her father's doctor with medical offices all over London.

Eki had told her father she couldn't remember the child's father because it all happened while she was asleep. Her story was simple: she wasn't raped but thought she was dreaming when the shit happened. Her father was furious but has no choice but to protect her only child and his own dignity . . .

In fact, she knew the boy responsible for her pregnancy. The reputation and status of her parents wouldn't allow her to disclose the identity of a one night stand (or maybe five-night stands) that shattered her dreams of having a child for Oko, the soccer star.

Her parents' loud mouth housemaid, Elizabeth, who knew all about it, even after she was sworn to secrecy, later told her gardener/husband, Judas, that Eki has been sleeping with her father's young chauffeur, a first cousin.

Oko had his own repertoire of women too. He was known to have different girls each day of the week. Many of them were disappointed because they couldn't fuck him on days he must show up for soccer practice. His mother had warned him to grow up and stop running around with so many girls.

On the one hand, his father, his devoted fan, and a polygamous man with a couple of his own concubines, was elated and proud of his son and his accumulation of girls. In one instance, his father was rumored to have kept girls for hours at his parlor and bedroom until his first son, Oko, was done with the one on his menu. As a point of reference, Oko's way with girls could be compared with one American legendry basketball super star from the south east.

At the age of twenty two, while stationed in the Republic of Benin, Oko fell in love with a beautiful village girl, Rachel Osika, who hailed from Efu in the eastern part of Nigeria. Rachel was just fifteen. Oko was young, in love, naïve, and clueless to Rachel's traditional courtship and protocol.

At the age of twenty-three, eight months, and five days old, to be exact, Oko's sweet girl, Rachel, gave birth to a bouncing baby boy. It was a joyous occasion for him. It was a joyous and sad occasion for her.

Oko never knew the reason his young beautiful girlfriend, the mother of his first child could be sad with the birth of their child. He saw the pain in her eyes. He was too stupid to see the cause of it. He had failed to accept that her pain and sadness were the result of his disregard for her culture, tradition, and his adamant belief in his new found western education and philosophy about marriage.

On the one hand, Rachel knew the birth of their son was the beginning of the end.

In earnest, they gathered their few belongings and headed to Efu to pay homage and present their new son, Okoro, to Rachel's family and the community at large. They took the risky 655 miles journey from the Republic of Benin in a sardine-packed lorry. Even though they arrived safely, Rachel's family reception was cold and unwelcomed, most especially to Oko, who was not only considered a stranger, but might have brought bad omens to their family and the whole village.

To voice their disdain for him, he was not allowed into Rachel's family house of Okpabi Osika.

In no uncertain terms, Chief Osika gave her daughter two choices: "You can go back with him and never return to this family because you have shamed me and my family or you can stay here in your father's house with your son without his father."

Within minutes of their arrival, words went out to family elders. The traditional leaders of the extended family gathered and brought with them items to appease the ancestors for the bad omens brought by one of their own daughters: seven kegs of palm wine, seven cola nuts, seven garden eggs, seven red peppers, seven bitter kola-nuts, seven yams, seven white hens, and seven he-goats.

They chanted, evoked the names of their ancestors, and prayed to them for protection. Most especially, they wanted the ancestors to drive away the evil spirit brought by Rachel and her illegitimate child. In addition, they scolded Rachel for bringing shame to their family, the same way her mother, Kulinkuli, did twenty one years ago when her eldest son was born before marriage. The son hasn't been seen for the last seventeen years. Several villagers, who came home for the Christian holidays or to attend traditional festivals, swore they sighted him in a white man's land.

To further appease the gods, the Supreme Leader of the family clan, Red Hat Chief Isaac Nwobodo, enumerated the list of items Rachel's mother, who had given birth to her "Devil's daughter, Rachel," must provide within seven days for the appeasement of the deities.

They included:

> *One he-goat, two she-goats, twenty-four kola nuts, two kegs of palm wine, ten tubers of dried yams, one bush meat, one bottle of palm oil, three handfuls of salt, ten bitter kolas, fifteen thousand Naira (about one hundred dollars), two white-feather hens, one white ram or four goats (if white ram couldn't be found), two dried fish, and other items that couldn't be spoken in public: they included herbs of various combinations from the deep forest.*

Rachel's father will be in charge of the herbs. In their family customs and traditions, men are in charge of the herbs . . .

On the seventh day, villager and family members gathered because they knew another feast was on the horizon. Regardless of the reasons for the gathering, multitude attended the festivities. It was the tradition. Within hours of the promised day, villagers in their best attire, gathered to denounce Rachel's act. That was the tradition by anyone who wanted to participate in the feast. They danced a little, chanted a lot, and ate the delicacies after the ancestral worship. As usual, in such affairs, all villagers and family members brought extra empty calabash dishes to take home their allotted portion of food and any leftovers.

After appeasing the deity by incantations, libation, and dancing for nearly three hours, Red Hat Chief Nwobodo called Rachel to kneel down with her mother, Kulinkuli, in front of the family and ask for forgiveness from the ancestors and the family elders. Kulinkuli was the third wife of Chief Osika.

Kulinkuli was particularly scolded and reminded once again how the native doctor had advised her husband, Chief Osika, against marrying her for the same blasphemy.

At that time, Chief Osika ignored the native doctor's advice not to marry her. The stubborn Osika wanted Kulinkuli for her beauty. He wanted her to be his third wife by any means. Moreover, she would be another helping hand on the family farm. Love had nothing to do with it. What's more, it would have been an insult to Osika not to possess a lady he wanted, at any cost. After all, he was the village Red Chief. He was the alpha and omega. He was THE OSIKA.

History just repeated itself once again. Kulinkuli had been asked to perform the same rituals with her own mother just as her daughter, Rachel, must now do with her. They were now considered the bearers of bad omens befalling the family and the village in recent history.

"Like mother like daughter," was the comment among Osika's family clan, especially by the light-skin seventy-seven year old niece who is known to foretell the future. Unfortunately, she hadn't seen this one coming.

Everyone in the village was now convinced of the native doctor's public predictions twenty seven days ago that a mother and her daughter were responsible for the sufferings encountered by their village to-date. The native doctor was certain it couldn't come from the Osika family. It wasn't supposed to happen twice in the same family within two scores and seven years.

The bad omens besieging them could now be blamed on the actions of Rachel, her boyfriend, and their illegitimate son. These omens included but not limited to:

The abnormal dry season . . .

The bad yam harvest from the Okeke village, seven miles away . . .

The lorry accident a few months ago in which twenty bearded goats were killed . . .

The village headmaster's second wife who gave birth to another daughter instead of twin boys as predicted by the light-skin old lady . . .

The fact that the eldest son of the Baptist church catechist married a white woman from a foreign land, instead of the postmaster's beautiful slender and beautiful daughter, Joyama.

The reason an 87-year old village chief couldn't impregnate his twenty-two year old sixth wife . . .

The reason the Chief Priest's daughter, who had been prearranged for marriage at the age of seven ran away at the age of nineteen to marry her high school sweet heart, somewhere in the capital . . .

The reason three hens belonging to a light-skinned woman from the far end of the village were killed by a drunk motorcyclist, on the village's market day . . .

The reason an Indian pam oil trader married a girl from his homeland instead of the beautiful village girl bequeathed to him with two cows and three goats by her father, a primary school headmaster, and the village's journalist and publisher . . .

The reason a Marijuana-pot-smoking son of a self-proclaimed pastor went mad . . .

> The reason the last born of the village Voodoo priest had six toes on his right foot and a protruded tooth . . .

> The reason Chief Osika's new-born had a dark skin and birth marks like his uncle . . .

A native son, visiting from United Kingdom asked one of the elders, "Would it have made a difference if they had not come home with the baby or not come home at all?" The only response by the elder to the innocent London visiting student was, "Quiet Osame, and mind your own business."

Nearly everyone kept their distance from Rachel and her son. Oko was later chased out of the village entirely. He thereafter took refuge in the adjacent village, forty seven miles away, at the home of a rival chief, until he could resolve his dilemma.

The medicine man, chanting traditional incantations and Christian prayers interchangeably, reminded the village chief, the Red Hat Chief Nwobodo that he had predicted these omens thirty fours days ago at the shrine sacrifice, but his warnings fell on deaf ears, and adequate steps weren't taken. According to the medicine man, the gods are still unhappy with the village people and their offerings presented thus far. As far as he is concerned, everyone in the village will suffer the consequences of Rachel's misjudgments and disregard for tradition.

The villagers shouted in one voice, "Tell us what to do, and we will do it, Chief Ogbanje, the medicine man."

The villagers realized the consequences of their disobedience and are ready to repent and sacrifice their worldly possessions to appease the gods. The medicine man thereafter proclaimed, "I'll give the oracle's temporary answers in seven minutes."

Still on their knees, Rachel and her mother ate the blessed seven kola nuts, one from each member of the village's seven elders. As instructed, they spit the chewed kola-nut into the air as mother and daughter remained half naked on the mud floor of their thatched dome-shaped hut, next to the ancestral shrine.

Although Osika's entire household were functionally Christians, they also consulted and prayed to their deity and ancestors on matters of this sort. White man's religion has its limitations, all of the time, in the Osika's household and the rest of the village.

So far, all the ancestry worshiping did not seem to be effective. After seven minutes, the medicine man came back with another revelation, "The family elders must fast for seven more days before the ultimate answers from the gods and their ancestors."

The feast for the occasion at hand belongs to the women and children, however. Only the goats will be smoked and be consumed with pounded yam and okra soup during the final rituals in another seven days by the elders.

Seven days later, the leaders of the family, Red Hat Chief Nwobodo, announced the medicine man's verdict: "Rachel, you're forbidden to go back with Oko under any circumstances."

"This would be the last time the name Oko would be spoken in this family," added one of the elders. The gods had spoken. The ancestors had sanctioned it.

To the elders, Rachel really had no say or choice in the matter.

Their reason was very simple: Rachel had committed the first cardinal rule, never to bear children before marriage. From that day forward, her son, who is now considered a bastard by default, would now be the official son of Rachel's father, Chief Osika.

Oko did all he could to appeal to the family to reconsider their decision through the elders in the adjacent village. The adjacent villager also wanted their own sacrificial items to appease their own gods before any intervention. Oko provided all they requested with no resolution.

He appealed to his country's diplomatic mission who failed to win back his son as well. The powers that be working on his behalf were African originals too. Africans will always be Africans. If the truth be told, the consulate office didn't really intervene in such cultural matters—too close to home.

Rachel had no choice but to stay with her son in her father's house according to custom and tradition. Otherwise, something tragic, including the death of her son within seven days would be unavoidable. What's more, Rachel would be paralyzed from her waist down, and be barren for life.

As further punishment, Rachel's mother would be reminded to the detached house at the back of the family compound. She would also be forced to remain within the compound, inside her hut, for seven days and without sex with her husband for another thirty seven days thereafter. The last restriction was not a concern for Chief Osika; he had two other wives and a concubine who were willing to serve him as required and when necessary. Polygamy had its benefits . . . Welcome to Nigeria of yester-years. Welcome to Nigeria of today. Welcome to Nigeria of tomorrow.

Yes, even though the household of Rachel's father was devoted to the house of the Lord with matters at hand, traditional beliefs would always prevail. Traditions die hard if they ever die at all, in that part of the universe.

Rachel was warned again, for the last time, by the family elders in their native tongues, "Take away the child and he would die in seven days and you will be barren."

To-date, Oko has not seen his son or known his whereabouts.

Rachel had warned Oko against his disdain for tradition but he was too stubborn to listen. His new found western education and white man's religion had beclouded his sense of cultural morality and judgment.

Oko's first son had since been renamed Omo-Ale Okpabi Osika. Omo-Ale means a bastard child. The poor boy, without his fault, was forever branded . . .

Oko's only hope was that his son will find him when he comes of age. The chance of that hope being fulfilled was one in a thousand. Traditions prevail forever in that part of the country. Even King Solomon wouldn't have had the power to overrule the verdict. Their gods had spoken.

If Oko had done his homework, he would have known that before any serious commitment to any girl from Efu, leaders in his family, preferably his father and uncle, should have first met with the Rachel's father and obtain permission before any relationship, and definitely before bearing any children. His failure to do so was a taboo especially when such disregard for her culture is by a man who does not even hail from her clan. The consequences of which were always devastating . . .

His resolve to do things his way, his determination to do things by his new indoctrinated civilized way, as taught to him at his Anglican missionary secondary school, and his stubbornness to defy his family tradition to marry his kind from Kurumbe, would later cost him dearly for the rest of his life.

Cultural conflicts had always been part of Oko's life. His marriage to his current wife, Beatrice, was a prearranged marriage by his parents. He had no choice in the selection. It was a matter of another culture. It was a matter of another tradition. As a matter of fact, his past encounters and experiences with his former girlfriend, Rachel, the mother of his first son, now called Omo-Ale, convinced him to obey his parents, this time around.

To him, when it rains, it pours. In fact, he had been standing in the middle of the rain all his life.

Although unconfirmed, rumor had it that his current wife was previously prearranged to be married to his older half-brother, Okorikori, before his own disappearance on his way from the family farm on a windy Friday, before his wedding day. No one knew for sure, to this day, if his half-brother ran away on his own accord to avoid the prearranged marriage he had told his friends and mother countless times he never wanted.

He had refused the marriage because the bride was not circumcised according to the native customs. His mother reminded him about this fact and pleaded with him to demand the circumcision or else . . . His father disagreed. Many in the village, on the other hand, believed to this day, that he was kidnapped, in broad daylight, and sacrificed by the native medicine men for the village's annual rituals. The latter was a rumor but no one in the village was ready or willing to dispute the story as told.

When Oko finally returned from Congo, no one told him about the whole affair surrounding his half-brother's disappearance or that their prearranged marriages were to the same woman.

A couple of his cousins joked with him about the arrangement on one or two occasions when they were intoxicated by a two-day old local palm wine, a bowl of pounded yam, and mixed okra and vegetable soup with bush meat and mushroom. Unbeknownst to him, he was paying for the food and local wine to be told the dark side of his past.

His torment from his relatives about his wife, real or not, her infidelity with his best friend, Dudu, and his resolve to seek a better life, were major contributing factors in his determination to emigrate to the United States.

He just wanted to get away, to anywhere but Kumasi, Ghana.

On June 9th, he left for the United States of America hoping never to return to the land of his birth.

Upon his arrival in the United States, he admired everything God's own country had to offer: paved roads, running water, uninterrupted electricity, the liberal educational system, the junk food, crime, discrimination, prejudice, many children disrespecting their parents, many parents equally disrespecting their children, some parents' inability to properly raise their children, high divorce rate, corruption by many, religious immorality, and shameless killings of innocent citizens.

He admired the country's good citizens, bad citizens, and many that are indifferent.

He loved those that fought for the poor. He was excited by the powerful few who fought for the rich and many people who do not give a fuck (I beg your pardon) about anything or anyone.

He wanted to be like many who were affectionate and cared on a daily basis for the power-less even when the powerless were unwilling to empower themselves because they turned deaf ears to their shortcomings—they are used to blaming others for everything under the sun.

He was proud of the country's military might and the economics of war it produces, in the name of peace, power, and territorial integrity.

He loved all the country's social programs benefitting the rich more than the poor they were designed for: food stamps programs, housing programs, and education programs, to name just a few. All in the name of what could be described as "Democratic capitalism," he once wrote in his private journal and soon to be published article.

He loved the American Constitution that bonded its democracy together: the Democratic Party, the Republican Party, and those that called themselves Independents. He wondered how anyone could be independent without an independent party. To him, they were nothing but former or undecided Democrats and Republicans because in the end, they voted as Democrats or Republicans or not at all. "Voting any other ways is a waste of vote," he wrote on page one hundred and fourteen in his journal.

He couldn't comprehend, however, how a country where the right to vote, fought with the blood and tears of many, and yet, less than forty-five percent of its citizens vote in nearly all elections.

He admired all the movements: the Tee Parti, the occupy Wall Street, and those fighting against abortion. In the end, some of the same anti-abortionist don't accept "Thou shalt not kill" as part of their ten commandments. They embraced, "An eye for an eye," instead.

"Only in America," he told himself, is where the good co-exist with the bad so perfectly.

He dreamt of becoming an American citizen one day, however.

He loved all Americans flaunting their wares. Yes, he admired the sexy women in particular. He deliberately turned on the news each morning and discovered that all news is now entertainment and all entertainment is now news. Weather news is now chic so are the infomercial selling snake oil to the vulnerable.

He loved all women of all races. He thought many were overweight but juicy nonetheless, as they bounced gracefully with their big butt and boobs. Sadly for him, such sights will never grace the roads of his dusty village, definitely not as packaged.

He saw countless others he considered perfectly fit, achieving their perfection through exercises, diet pills, liposuctions, and tummy tucks. Many became what they became by all means legal or otherwise—natural ways are no longer part of the equation.

He loved how Americans exhibit their sexuality and its economic impact. He had studied that aspect in his microeconomics class.

Before he totally committed himself to the Lord and considered himself born again to the American way, he visited many strip joints and saw capitalism of the flesh at work. Yes, he was aroused and tempted many times. He wasn't proud that he succumbed once to the tentacles of the devil in New York City. Ok, maybe more than once. He hadn't kept good records of his actions for reason only known to him. He had confessed privately his sins to his Lord and had been forgiven. Matters closed.

He just could not understand how a religious country like the United States of America would tolerate such decadence. He had seen evils of the flesh by genuine Americans in San Diego, Atlantic City, New York, Maryland, Washington DC, in his own city, Richmond, Virginia, and on the internet.

On the other hand, he saw many of his fellow Church members patronizing these sinful establishments. "I'll pray for their souls," was all he could say. Maybe they should pray for his soul too.

If he had his way and had the ruthless raw power like the oppressive leaders in his native land, he would eradicate all flesh for sale ventures. He wouldn't hesitate sending their promoters and stakeholders of these immoral ventures to a long term jail sentences. Even, a select few would be sent to the death chambers just as proposed by church leaders for homosexuals in some African countries. It will serve as a reminder to generations to come of the mighty arms of his God to befall anyone with such evil acts and thoughts.

Maybe, he wouldn't go that far, it's tempting nonetheless. At least, not when he wanted to make United States his permanent home. "Such actions may come back to haunt me," he told himself. According to him, America has taken freedom of speech and expression too far.

In his village, the old and not so old women walked around exposing their breasts everywhere while their young daughters anxiously displayed their pointed nipples, firm breasts, and butt to entertain visiting foreign dignitaries in the name of culture, during festivals and official functions, at no cost.

He had read in Playboy magazine and the like, where women or men were paid exorbitant prices just for showing their breasts and other body parts.

In America, the display of the flesh was big business and profitable ventures. Some called such enterprises sexual exploitation, others called it freedom, and many considered it works of art.

He read about former Playboy playmates, some of whom became movie stars. Some were rumored to have had affairs with former presidents, former presidential candidates, Senators, politicians, businessmen, religious leaders, and famous musicians.

He envied the capitalism of the American citizens; even though he might disagree with the means they are achieving it.

In his native land, body parts are shown free of charge, but in this great country of Washington, Jefferson, Martin Luther King, Jr., George W. Bush, and the main man, Barrack Obama, the flesh was money making enterprise. He admired the economic benefits of free enterprises.

"Fuck the African cultures," he said aloud as he considered the majority of his African cultures and traditions as uneconomical, regressive, and unproductive.

"Only in America is where all things are possible," he told himself, again and again.

What troubled him was very simple: the greatness of America was what he considered its flaws. To him, the good and the bad are two sides of the same coin.

With prayers, he would overcome these temptations. Unlike Jesus Christ, he had failed the temptations tests.

Then, he recalled Luke 4:1-9:

And Jesus being full of the Holy Ghost returned from Jordan, and was led by the Spirit into the wilderness, being forty days tempted of the devil. And in those days he did eat nothing: and when they were ended, he afterward hungered. And the devil said unto him, if thou be the Son of God, command this stone that it be made bread. Jesus answered him, saying, it is written, that man shall not live by bread alone, but by every word of God.

And the devil, taking him up into a high mountain, showed unto him all the kingdoms of the world in a moment of time. And the devil said unto him, all this power will I give thee, and the glory of them: for that is delivered unto me; and to whomsoever I will give it. If thou therefore wilt worship me, all shall be thine. And Jesus answered and said unto him, get thee behind me, Satan: for it is written, Thou shalt worship the Lord thy God, and him only shalt thou serve.

And he brought him to Jerusalem, and set him on a pinnacle of the temple, and said unto him; if thou be the Son of God, cast thyself down from hence.

Oko would have failed even the first test.

CHAPTER 8

The second time Oko laid eyes on Precious was on a spring day in his advanced religion research class. He was in his third year in the country. He was happy to be back in school if only he would be able to see Precious alive and well. When he saw her, he couldn't summon the courage to approach her. Maybe, it was the engagement ring on her finger or it might have been as a result of his present circumstances. He was nonetheless overwhelmed by her beauty as always. She dressed and walked to kill. She bounced like a famous Hollywood diva auditioning for R-rated movie roles. Her maker did her justice, any day, anytime, perfectly . . .

Many times thereafter, during class meetings, they nodded at each other at a distance and went their separate ways like total strangers on the street of New York.

As usual, Precious continued to receive many more letters from her admirer. She was anxious to read them each day when Jeremy was away on church missions or at therapy sessions. She considered her actions as a fantasy and an innocent affair. The down side was that the attention she was getting from her admirer had made the reconciliation process with her fiancé, Jeremy, more difficult if not impossible.

One Friday evening, after work, she received the following letter from her admirer:

"Please, know this . . . I woke up this morning and discovered that I'm the best for you. I looked into the mirror and saw what many near and afar see about me. I've decided to celebrate me. Allow me to share with you a few of my attributes."

I am:

Handsome
Hardworking
Cute
Responsible
Dependable
Caring
Considerate
Giving
Handsome
Tolerant
Intelligent
Creative and talented
Well built
Great dresser
Uncompromising
Great cook
Clean and well groomed
Financially promising
Raised with great personal habits
Handsome . . . did I mention that already? Oh, well.
Intelligent . . . this is worth repeating
I am humble
Good looking . . . not quite handsome but better.
But I have an unresolved problem: I want you to
share in my attributes.

"Hope I made your day. Smile. You're so beautiful."

For better or for worse, she had met her match. "Was the son-of-a-bitch, humble, arrogant or what?" She said to herself. If her feeling of the admirer was right, she knew it must be a forbidden path she must tread gently. His creativity is drawing her nearer and nearer, to him unwillingly.

That evening, she couldn't sleep. At 3:15 in the morning, she took out all the mails, cards, and sketches of her from her stranger-admirer. Logic and rationalization were becoming rare commodities in her mindset.

"Why was he so much on my mind? Was it because I had not had sex within twenty four hours?" she asked herself.

She had had enough. She jumped into the shower, put on her favorite old skimpy two-piece lingerie underneath her coat, ran into her car, and drove directly to Jeremy's efficiency apartment.

When she opened the door, Jeremy was reading Matthew 5.

Yes, she had her own key to his apartment. On the other hand, he didn't have the key to her house. In her word, fairness is how she defines it.

As she opened the door, Jeremy attempted to hug her. All she said to him was, "Jay, do your thing and fuck me."

"May I lick you a little this evening?" Jeremy nervously asked.

Jeremy even got the time of the day confused. It was 4:45 in the morning. The power of Precious over him was now an addiction. He was fucked and incoherent. In colloquial terms, "He was pussy whipped."

"Not today. Just fuck me," she fired back.

She left immediately thereafter with only, "Thank you, Jay. See you later."

Girlfriend just wanted to be fucked. Affection was no longer in her dictionary when Jeremy is the receiving party.

She never used dildos, not when live dick was at her disposal. Jeremy was always available for full service and on demand.

On her way home, listening to Billy Holidays' *These Foolish Things*, reminded her of her relationship with Jeremy to-date.

"That's the problem with Jay. He is weak, obedient, and sexually mediocre. However, he is loyal and dependable . . . Shit I just missed my turn," she said, as she turned back to her upper middle class housing development.

Getting home, she took her shower, tucked inside her satin sheet, butt naked, and went over her admirer's latest notes she had left in her bed earlier in the evening. Her nipples stood erect. She squeezed them gently with one hand and played with her clit with her left middle finger, and imagined how it would feel if the admirer was making love to her instead.

She turned off the lights and contemplated in the dark, "If he came to me right now, I would fuck him. What will be mine will be mine," she said as she dozed off with a smile on her face.

The next day, a dozen white roses were delivered to her office. The accompanying note, although unsigned, contained the following: "White is pure as you're. Anyone who could maintain white in any form is the richest person in the world. I'll maintain it. I'll keep it shining. You're my white flower."

Under any other circumstances, she would've considered the attention she was getting as stalking and called for police protection. In this case, she recognized the admirer as harmless and innocent child of God just trying to express love. On instinct, she walked to her office window and saw the admirer as he drove away in a car she recognized a few times on campus. "That's Mr. Oko. I knew it" she said with a smile.

Her suspicion had been on target all along. In fact, they'd seen each other every week on their way to classes. They usually acknowledged each other just as much as they pretended to ignore one another.

Before all the notes, portrait sketches, and flowers from him, she had told herself numerous times, "It wasn't right to mess with this man, if he turned out not to be the one for me."

Even if all went well, even if she had to eat the forbidden fruit, even if her life will fit perfectly together with him, if Jeremy wasn't to be considered in the equation, and even if Riodiaz had not fucked up, she was determined to give Jeremy another chance. At times, she wants to have a conscience, courtesy of Pastor Shackle.

Pastor Shackles had advised her in no uncertain terms to give Jeremy a chance. "He is a devoted and loving man of God, please give him a chance," he told her countless times.

At this juncture, her only option was to ignore her secret lover. "Or maybe, a bite of the apple just one time wouldn't hurt. After all, Adam ate the forbidden fruit and lived," she told herself. The tide of self-control was turning against her resolve . . .

Two days later, she received a full-length sketch of herself receiving her diploma along with one stem rose with this note:

> *I wanted to congratulate you on your graduation*
> *yesterday. I knew you felt relieved and joyous for*

your efforts and achievements. You've accomplished so much without complaint. I'm proud of you.

I'm sure you also knew I obtained my first degree as well. As a result, I will be traveling to my home land to visit my parents and at the same time take care of some family affairs. I should be back within four weeks. I hope you think of me while I'm away. I'll be thinking of you. Since I'm not privileged to your email address or telephone, I wouldn't be able to communicate with you, except give you a shout out on Facebook.

Here is how I captured you as you received your diploma yesterday. To me, capturing you in digital wouldn't do you any justice. Leonardo da Vinci didn't paint the Mona Lisa and the Last Super in Polaroid. Michelangelo didn't paint the Sistine Chapel with Photoshop. Their works of art were all original.

To me, you must be painted in the original. I'm the master artist of your original.

He also sent her one of his favorite poems from Vanessa Obioha's collection of poems, titled "Crazy feelings."

The thoughts of you kept me awoke most nights. I feel obsessed by your beauty. Like opium, I'm addicted to you

*I stay up late to hear you sing from your window
I hid in the dark just to watch your hips sway
What can I do to make you come and stay?
You have ignited a burning flame in me
It's so ablaze with a raw desire for you*

You have captured my soul in a weird way
There is a desperate longing for you
My words may seem empty to you

How I wish it was possible to paint my love for you
To sing to the birds my endless passion for you
To whisper to the stars how your beauty dazzles me
You are my dandelion
So glad you strayed to my heart
Hesitate no more
Feel the rush of my love for you in waves of the
deep blue sea. Hear my heartbeat in the rhythm of
the night

Give me a chance darling
Give me a chance to show you how much you mean
to me
I love you like no other
For in you I found real joy and happiness

Please my love, take me and use me as you wish
I want to be your humble servant
Let me be a fool for your love
For you have captured my soul
And make me a slave to love
For how else can I explain this crazy feeling?
This undying love for you

I love you
And I will keep on loving you
Till you free me from these crazy feelings.

Oko then added his last thought in another note:

"When I come back from my trip, I'll be moving into another apartment. I know you haven't seen my present one but I just want to keep you updated in case I'm graced to welcome you to my new abode. If you were to ask me what I would want before I travel tomorrow at 2:30pm out of Norfolk International Airport, I would simply say, I want a big hug and a juicy farewell kiss. I love you."

He wanted to use the words "I love you" the first day he saw her, but he had been told it was a taboo to use those three letter words in a relationship with African American women in the first phase of dating. It never made any sense to him. "These Americans and their crazy philosophy," he lamented.

Before Oko walked to the runway to board his plane, he looked back on instinct. At a distance, he saw Precious standing without any emotion, and probably saying, "Safe journey, O."

He waved goodbye without expecting reciprocity from her. He said to himself with a smile and with a sense of exoneration, "Thank you Jesus. I can't wait to be back." The thought of canceling his trip came to his mind. He just couldn't afford the financial alternative.

Precious drove back home with a sense of loneliness. Deep down, she missed him already. She was looking forward to reading his notes and admiring his daily sketches of her. "How long would I have these thoughts of him and how long would he be gone?" she asked herself. She took a deep breath and said, "This is just another phase of lust and nothing more, please help me Lord."

CHAPTER 9

Lolita got home later than usual and found her husband, Riodiaz waiting for her by the door.

Lolita: Good evening Diaz, (the name she called him to differentiate it from Rio, he was called by his ex-wife, Precious) I hope your trip went as planned. How are Alice and the children?

Diaz: They are doing fine. What about you? I've dinner ready, in case you're still hungry. (He can count on his fingers how many times he had been in the kitchen since their marriage)

Lolita: I had a bite already but I can join you at the table, if you prefer.

Diaz: Thanks. I want to talk to you.

Lolita: No problem. Let me change and I'll be back in a few seconds. Aside, she said, he always talked to me, not with me.

Diaz: Okay, babe.

She couldn't believe her ears. She couldn't remember the last time he called her babe. She went to her son's room, tucked him in comfortably, and kissed him goodnight. She bade the babysitter goodnight. She then put on a sexy white top revealing the shape of her slender body. As if to prove a point, she wore his favorite leopard pumps usually worn during the good times with him. She poured herself a glass of red wine, offered Diaz the same, and sat down at the other end of the table.

Lolita: Your food looks cold. Do you want me to warm it up for you?

Diaz: No thanks. I'm ok. Could you please sit closer? I want to talk to you. By the way, you look stunning . . . I hope you're not pregnant?

Lolita: Excuse me? (She frowned a little, moved closer, and sat across from him). Thanks for the compliment. FYI, I'm not pregnant. Maybe, only the Blessed Virgin Mary could be pregnant under our circumstances.

Diaz: (He ignored her comments, cleared his throat, and began). Lita, I know we've been distant for sometimes now. I know our divorce papers will be finalized soon. I know you consider yourself a model mother and wife. I also know things haven't been right between us for sometimes. I cannot pinpoint why we ended up this way, but, I'm ready to give you a chance to make things work. If not for our marriage, you must do it for our son, Michael.

My son deserves both parents and I'll try my best to make things work if you act right. I want you to withdraw the divorce papers. For this marriage to work, you must come home early each day and take care of your family. Your career should not be a priority at this early years of my son. That was one of the reasons I paid for your law school education.

Most of all, the babysitter will have to go. I'm not comfortable with the way she handled our son. Sometimes I wonder if she loves you more instead of taking care of our son. Your affair with her is none of my business. You're a mother and wife first and you should be able to do more to be in your son's life instead of chasing after a career.

A woman's job should be to stay at home and take care of her family. Your job is to do exactly that. Look at me Lita, I'm still speaking . . .

Maybe if you dress up more as you do tonight, you would get laid more often.

My daughter Alice, her partner, Samoa, and their children may be visiting us in about six weeks. I've told them they could stay as long as they want so that we could catch up for the time lost between us. (He then shifted in his seat, took a big bite of the macaroni and cheese and down a big gulp of his favorite dry red wine).

Once again, Riodiaz was convinced a woman's place is at home, pregnant and barefooted. He had never been able to handle the challenges of an intelligent, beautiful, and hard-working woman. He left his ex, Precious, after she decided to pursue graduate studies, among other things. "Women's lib was the beginning of the end of modern family as we know it," he reiterated.

Lolita: Have you finished, sir?

Diaz: Go ahead. I'm about done.

Lolita: Thanks for your lecture, daddy. By the way, how is Precious?

Diaz: She was fine. She sent her greetings.

Lolita: What about Alice and her children again? Did you say, "Her partner?"

Diaz: They are doing just fine. You already asked about them earlier. Thank you for repeating it.

Lolita: Diaz, I'm pleased you're home and well. Your son missed you. I heard all you said and all you had gracefully offered me. Thank you, sir. I couldn't have had a better father in my life. I hope you'll give me the same respect and hear me out as I had listened to you without interruption. Unlike you, I had ended this relationship and our marriage weeks ago. I never knew our marriage would end this way but it has. I've decided to move on and see where life takes me. I hope we can work . . .

Diaz stood up and interrupted her . . .

Diaz: Who the hell is the mother-fucker and . . . ?

Lolita: Excuse me, no need for foul language, please. Let me finish.
         If you don't, then I'm done.

Diaz: Shit, go ahead, Ms. Attorney Lolita Gilbert or whatever his fucking name is . . .

Lolita: I want you to be in our son's life. I want you to play a fatherly role with him unlike your daughter. I'll be moving out my things within thirty days. If you want me out sooner, that will be fine. Just let me know, please.

Diaz: Can I talk now?

Lolita: Sure, I'm done, sir.

Diaz: I bet you are running into the arms of your underage rich boyfriend, Frankie. I thought you're a Catholic and yet, you're sleeping with that adolescence, snobbish, and so called client of yours behind my back. Your behavior is pitiful and sickening. You haven't even allowed our dilapidated engine running our marriage to cool down before you started whoring around.

I know you're a lawyer; I'll not make it easy for you. Definitely, I'll seek custody of my son because I can prove you're not a fit mother. Not by a long shot. I have copies of your texts and e-mails to your toy boy as evidence of your infidelity. I thought you would be different. You're nothing but an ungrateful whore in a business suit. Precious wouldn't have done that to me and . . .

Lolita interrupted him this time.

"Diaz, thank you. Have a good evening. I'm done with you."

Riodiaz was caught unaware and did not expect Lolita's reaction to his new plan to jump start his sinking marriage after Precious had rejected him. Lolita had been obedient and compromising in the past. In a way, he had thought Lolita's obedience, devotion, and simplicity had given him the ammunition and the authority to do whatever he wanted. He thought he would remake his hibernated marriage, now that Precious had moved on. He was obviously mistaken. He was a proud man who refused to admit to his downfalls . . .

Lolita had done the same as his ex, Precious, and moved on even faster than he could imagine. He had denied his reality. He had thought Lolita would consider his proposition under any circumstances. His pride and stupidity by any definition had led him to the abyss.

He then enumerated the three strikes against him: His ex, Precious had rejected him. His current, soon-to-be ex, for all practical purposes, just left him. He would soon say goodbye to his son. Once again, he had come face to face with his past, his future, or whatever the case may be.

Exactly one week thereafter, Lolita moved out of their house before Riodiaz came back from work. She moved to a studio apartment owned by one of her colleagues at her law firm. Her divorce would also be handled by one of her law partners. Riodiaz would've paid handsomely for the divorce, but all Lolita wanted was her freedom and custody of their son. She got that freedom and a joint custody in 90 days after their separation.

Riodiaz had walked away from his daughter. This time, he had lost the son he desperately wanted to raise with all the love in him.

That evening, with her divorce papers in hand, Lolita spoke with Frank for almost five hours. Frank recognized in her voice that she is happy but wanted her to tell him herself the source of her happiness.

Lolita just wanted to talk about Frank and his day. She would have liked him to pick her up, except for the fact that her husband is at home. She never told him about her new studio apartment or that her divorce was final. Seductively, she joked, "My love, come and pick me up or talk to me all night . . ." Frank knew that coming to pick her up wasn't an option.

They always enjoyed each other's company. They clicked in every way possible. They made sure they enjoyed every moment together. They custom made their love. They bonded with love, passion, and mutual happiness.

They accepted each other as an individual with respect and dignity. As he always told her, "Love should never be with tears."

She remembered her past and was conscious not to repeat the painful part, as she reminded herself many times the old saying, "Those who forget history are bound to repeat it." She supported his views and vowed to have his back. She recognized their differences and admired their strengths. To her, they were the only two people in her universe.

For his part, Frank cherished her simplicity, intellect, and beauty. He envied her energy, sense of humor, and sense of sensibility. "Fun to be with was her best part," he always said to himself.

As he reminiscence his love for her, he almost shed tears when he shared what he called "The peace she gave me," to his close friends.

"I'm her king. She is my queen. We are the only people who matter in this world," he had told his grandfather every Sunday at family dinner. During one of those dinners, his grandfather had asked him, "Frankie, tell me in less than ten words, why you are in love with your lady?"

"She gives me peace of mind, grandpa," he replied.

He had described the love of his life in seven words.

The key to their comfort was their positive admiration for each other, the respect for one another, and their conscious resolve to do what it takes to make their relationship work. It was their custom-made relationship and not a preprogramed relationship as defined by others that makes their love special and fun.

They listen to each other with respect and understanding. They recognize their natural roles in their union. Each time they get together, they talk mostly about themselves and complement each other. They refused to carry over the events of the day at work into their limited but valuable time together. Lolita once wrote to him:

> Let's make sure no one or anything comes between us. When our story is written, we will be described as lovers made for each other by the Lord Almighty.

And she concluded with Songs of Solomon 8:7:

> *Many waters cannot quench love, nor will rivers overflow it; if a man were to give all the riches of his house for love, it would be utterly despised.*

Two days later, Lolita and Frank flew to Belize to celebrate his birthday and also conducted some businesses in the process. Frank had an excellent team of corporate certified public accountants and tax attorneys who knew the loopholes to get a full deduction for such trip as business expenses. America and its tax loopholes . . . Awesome!

Everywhere they went—business meetings, restaurants, hotels, and parks, people perceived them as a loving and happy couple. Jokingly, Frank would turn around and say to her, "See, everyone thought we were married already. We're the only one clueless at our reality."

As they sat in bed after dinner, Frank turned to Lolita, kissed her softly, and said, "Love, I have a great idea. Would you like to be married in two countries the same day?

"My love, how could that be possible," she responded.

"My sweetheart, I can make it happen, you know, I'm the man with the plan" he said with a smile.

"My love, first thing first, I have to see the Monsignor to obtain his permission to remarry, if you still want to marry me," she said.

He was, for some reason, extremely jolly since the beginning of the week. He called Lolita's cell phone; she refused to pick it up. She wanted to surprise him of her good news.

He rushed home to call Lolita but was happily surprised to see her at his doorsteps welcoming him home with a smile and flowers.

On his doorsteps, she knelt in front of him and said, "My darling, I love you and there is no man on the face of this earth I cherish more than you. I'm free. I'm yours if you still want to have me. Today, I'm a virgin once again. I'm now your only virgin: clean, fresh, whole, willing, and ready to be your queen."

Within three months of Lolita's divorce, Monsignor gave his blessing to Lolita's request to remarry. Earlier in the day, Frank had felt it in his bones that everything was just right the entire day.

As she started to cry, Frank held her up and led her inside and unto the couch. He licked the drops of tears from her beautiful face and said, "My love, I have now drank your blessed water, and together we are one."

They started kissing. This time, it was not the same as before but better. The kiss was passionate. It was peaceful. It was as if it has been blessed from the heavens. They knew the day was different. Softly, in her usual style, Lolita said, "Darling, please make love to me. I'm all yours now."

He looked at her, kissed her one more time, smiled, and rested his head on her chest.

As he palmed her breasts, he said, "Darling, I'm grateful for your love. I'm dying to make love to you but I'm going to do it right. We had waited this long, we can wait for our special day."

Lolita then changed position, knelt with one knee, brought out an engagement ring she had carried with her for three and half months, and said, "Frank, would you bestow on me your grace and be my husband?"

Still crying, she continued: "My love, the few months we've been together have been the best in my life. You've made me whole so much so that I hardly remember the sad parts of my past. You're my king. There is nothing more in my life I wouldn't give up to be your everlasting queen. Just today . . ."

Interrupting her, Frank kissed her tenderly, deep, and long . . . and said, "My love, let me answer your questions first, so that I can be safe you're mine?"

"Yes. Yes. I'll be your husband for the rest of my life."

She was wet, hot, and ready to make love with him. He refused. She understood.

The next Friday afternoon, they arranged an overnight babysitter to take care of her son. They flew in his corporate jet to New Delhi to have her favorite food, "Tandoori" and later jetted to the French Riviera for a well-planned wedding, Saturday morning.

Frank had planned it for months. He had always been a man of confidence. After the weeding merriments, they jetted back to his parents' home on the hills of West Virginia, for the second wedding, the same Saturday evening. Six hours' time zone differences made it all possible.

They'd just gotten married twice on the same day. Cool. Frank, the man, made it happen.

Even though few were invited, many came to the wedding of Mr. & Mrs. Gilbert.

Her ex, Mr. Riodiaz was there by obligation since his company was the local TV station covering the events under the variety section on the 6 o'clock news on channel FGTV 6. Frank's family owns the station. For all practical purposes, they owned Riodiaz.

Frank specifically requested for Riodiaz to cover the wedding to see what he would be missing for the rest of his life. "What a loser," Frank said to himself.

It was the best wedding since Prince Charles and Diana, except that Frank Gilbert was no Charles, the Prince of Edinburgh, and Lolita was no Diana, the TV darling. As they tell it, their wedding was better.

Although guests were streaming in to greet the newlyweds, Lolita had had enough of sharing such valuable time with the public instead of being with her husband working on her pussy.

She was hot and wet, mostly between her legs. Her nipples were hard. She was shaking and incoherent as she spoke with guests. Every time she shook anyone's hand, she wanted it to be Frank's dick ready to fuck her pulsating wet pussy.

On their first dance as a couple, she held him tight and kissed him.

As her breathing became heavy and uncontrollable, she simply said to him, "My husband, get me out of here and fuck me." She didn't give a fuck who may be listening. A few did actually.

Within seconds, they excused themselves and asked the master of ceremony to deliver the appropriate messages to the multitude at hand. After all, many of the guests were uninvited souls.

They disappeared like ghosts to those who weren't paying much attention.

They drove to the tenth floor of their five star hotel's bridal suites. Every inch of the room was covered with flowers of all sizes, shapes, and color. The center piece was flown in from Rio de Janeiro, a reminder of her birth place.

After three days of hibernation, all hotel staff was reliving the Robert Redford's 1967 movie, *Barefoot in the Park*. The only important difference was that they had modern technology to communicate to the outside world this time around.

They used Facebook and Twitter to communicate to a select few for a maximum of ten minutes per day, during sex break. To them, there was no world outside their world. Frank got all he ever wanted and more.

At one point, Lolita said, "My love, you filled me up so much, I think we may need to start picking our son's name in nine months." To which he joyfully said, "Darling, you beat me to that because I had twins in mind." She knew such personal love making could only result in one outcome: a blonde, blue-eye child just like him.

On their third day of self-imposed sex quarantine, Lolita discussed with Frank the result of his responses to her questionnaire. Ninety-one percent of his answers were compatible with hers.

Sample differences:

> *He was a Democrat. She was an independent libertarian, whatever that means.*

> *He wanted their children to go to private schools, she preferred public schools.*

> *He did not want quiet time to himself; she enjoyed "Me time" alone, once a week.*

Sample similarities:

> *They wanted passionate sex at least twice a week. They agreed to safe five hundred dollars a month if they had sex more than eight times a month, and safe one thousand dollars a month if they had sex less than*

*eight times a month. They called the account
"The $exucation funds."*

They love nasty sex. They cherish romance.

They loved children.

They were both social drinkers.

They hated snorting and sniffing.

*They fantasize about threesome but never
wanted to put it into practice.*

*They agreed LeBron James should've stayed
in Cleveland instead of defecting to the
Miami Heat. They just don't like the Florida
outfit. Lolita despised "The Heat" because
one of their star players was her high school
sweetheart who got married to someone else
after he became a super star. The same fellow
is now dating a movie star—she wouldn't
swear to this fact under oath. Frank, on the
other hand, dislikes the HEAT outfit because
his grandfather wasn't able to acquire the
franchise many years ago-an unnamed
billionaire from the valley won the bid.*

On the fifth day, as he did every morning, Frank made her a
cup of tea and slim biscuits in bed. He handed her an envelope
addressed to "My love, Lita." It was a deed in Lolita Gilbert's
name to a two-bedroom beach front condominium in Rio de
Janeiro.

"Honey, you have done enough. You have made me whole
and God is my witness. I'll serve you until death do us part. If

you would, please look under your pillow, I have for you my own little gift." It was a two bedroom condo at the Rotunda in Sarasota, Florida.

She then gave her a kiss and said, "I'm all yours forever. Thank you, my one and only love."

"My all, I don't want you to make the decision right now, but what do you think if we made the deeds in both our names? I would like what is yours or mine to be ours," she told him.

There were no prenuptial agreements, against his attorneys' recommendations. To both, love wouldn't be measured by the almighty dollar, the world's medium of exchange.

"Tomorrow, you can amend the deeds as you recommended since that is your area of expertise," Frank responded.

And they made love; Lolita was sore but tenderly sweet. She didn't want to stop the pleasure, however.

Frank wanted to recover from her all the love and sex he had denied himself. He wanted to unload all the "Reserve" in his arsenal, to-date. "Darling, it was worth the wait," he said aloud to his new bride.

"But you made me a Cinderella I never hoped to be. I love you," she replied.

"Honey, let's change the wet sheet."

"Of course not," he responded.

Heavens, their nasty sex has just begun.

CHAPTER 10

Oko could only reach Precious on Facebook. He sent sketches of her as promised each day. Her homepage was becoming an art gallery. She loved the attention from her temporary international admirer and globe trotter. Precious smiled every time she opened her Facebook every morning. Her Facebook friends were leaving messages asking "Precious, who is this O fellow? Girl, he sounds so fine." After many of similar comments, she sent Oko her private chat room.

One cold Saturday evening, she sent Oko a simple message, "Mr. Man, stay safe and come home soon."

Oko immediately changed his departure date to come back to the United States one week early to be closer to her, even though he was uncertain of what awaited him. He bade farewell to what was left of his family in Ghana and looked forward to the fresh love burning through his heart in the United States.

He came bearing gifts. By all accounts, Precious' gifts were sufficient to open a gallery of African Arts.

Poor Jeremy, he questioned the size and quantity of the artifacts. She quickly convinced him that she was planning to open a small business in African arts for sale on eBay. She couldn't believe she didn't tell Jeremy, her fiancé, the truth. For the first time, the love of Oko touched her heart, a man she hardly knew, and was ready and willing to lie about him. Translation: love.

Obviously, there was trouble in the love paradise between her and Jeremy. Their relationship counseling was at serious risk if more was not done to put it back on track. Subsequently, she found herself listing the negatives Jeremy possessed, to convince herself it's time for her to move on.

Since Riodiaz's departure, Oko was once again the center of her universe: he had the height. He had educational ambition. He had wisdom. He was artistic, romantic, strong, and like Riodiaz, his British accent in his native tongue was mesmerizing.

She had been taken by his physique, candor, intellect, kindness, respect, authoritative style, creativity, wisdom, and his originality. She knew she might fall in love with him if the time had been perfect. Timing was everything. Perfect timing wasn't on her side to-date.

Deep down, she continued to wonder if the tales about African men with naturally big long-fat-round-dick, and their stamina to fuck all-night long were true. She had dreamt of Oko making love to her with his presumed signature equipment like a jungle man. She dreamt sweet dreams about him and his ability to fulfill her everyday needs. She was known for one thing: she was always true to her sexual needs.

Upon returning to the United States, Oko intentionally refused to communicate with her on Facebook. He hated his decision to do so but wanted her to miss him. Yes, he was still a smooth operator.

He was right. She missed him more deeply than usual. She sent him messages on Facebook and wondered if he was ok. "O, hope you are enjoying your trip?" She really wanted the message to read, "My love, where the heck are you . . . let me hear from you, I'm lonely and waiting for you." She couldn't write those words. Not yet, at least. Not on social media for the whole world to read.

One late afternoon, Precious brought out her favorite wine and poured herself a full glass. After two glasses, she sat at the middle of her living room and folded her legs as if ready to do yoga or meditate. She placed her laptop on her lap and wanted to update her diary for the week. At the middle of Precious' narratives, she decided to play around and e-mail Oko through his school address. By now, Precious was mellow, tipsy, and wanted to express her suppressed feelings for him. Playing downstairs on her high fidelity Bose stereo system was the song, "Who let the dog out," by Baha men.

Send to: Okokediri@ibu.edu

From: Prie.diva.riodiaz.danford@phd.com

Subject: Bring your hot dog.

O, I've not heard from you for two days. What's up? I hope you're doing well. I never knew you would forget me so soon. Please, let me know when you will be returning to the States. I hope you haven't gone home and get married to one of your harem? I am sitting here alone thinking about you and wishing, if you are not too far away, I would've asked you to come and have me as your dinner tonight. Yes, I must confess, I can't take it without you anymore. I'm here all butt naked, playing with myself and wishing your tongue is all over me . . . , yes, you must lick me down there . . . I want you so bad O, I can't think straight. Take out your raw, naturally grown hot dog and do me. I want you to do me. I dreamt last night that you were doing me at your studio . . .

In the middle of Precious' e-mail, her cell rang. She attempted to answer it with her Skype. Mistakenly, she clicked the sent button on her incomplete e-mail to Oko instead. "Shit, shit, I didn't mean to do that," she said, as she quickly tried to unsent it. It was too late. Deep down, she missed Oko and probably would have sent him the e-mail when the right time presents itself. Deep down, Precious meant every word she wrote. She knew it wasn't the right time to say what she wanted to say, however. The glasses of wine brought out the reality in her. For heaven's sake, she has a live-in fiancé.

Precious poured the remaining wine into her glass, walked towards her bathroom, and said, "O well, the shit is gone now and I can't do anything about it."

Her good Lord was on her side. Her account with the Lord had a credit balance because forty five minutes later, Oko's e-mail was return as "Undeliverable." "Thank you Lord. I really need to catch up on my tithes," she said with a sigh of relief.

Oko's correct e-mail address is Okonkediri@ibu.edu

She wasn't joking, however, when she said none of the African queens deserved him. She was now becoming lovingly blind for a man she had admired from afar. Maybe love, after all, is actually blind at the beginning.

Oko had other pressing issues on his plate as well: he was working on registering for his graduate studies, finding paying job, and at the same time planning to bring his children back to the United States. His love for Precious had made matters more complicated. His student visa was extended for additional two years, restricted by scholarship agreement he signed with his home ministry to return to Ghana after graduate studies to assist his people.

He sent a message back to Precious on Facebook telling her that he would be home in another two hours, even though he had been home for a week. All of a sudden, she was nervous and wondering if she should go shopping for a new wardrobe. "Fuck, what's wrong with me? He is just an acquaintance. We don't even have a date," she said with a chuckle. She reluctantly went shopping, nonetheless.

When Precious returned, she received another package from Oko. She smiled and rejoiced to the fact that Oko hadn't forgotten her. Inside the package, Precious found a teddy bear and a fertility doll with a note, "Please, use the teddy bear to stay warm at night. The other was to show my seriousness and commitment."

She loved the teddy bear but was not sure about the fertility doll. It had been nearly nineteen years since she gave birth to her daughter, Alice.

Riodiaz tried before their divorce to have more children without success. Jeremy continued the endeavor but fell short to-date.

Precious smiled and told herself, "Don't hold your breath, lover boy. Children are out of the question."

She did the numbers and was convinced fertility doll is a myth and definitely not on her horizon. "These Africans and the Voodoo shit," she said aloud.

Precious slept peacefully all night and couldn't wait to lay eyes on Oko in their advanced humanity class . . .

The following evening, she went to Jeremy's apartment for her usual sexual fix. I beg your pardon; she actually described her scheduled visit to Jeremy's temporary abode as, "Her sexual needs and his obligations."

This time around, Precious wanted to be fucked with her clothes on. As always, she got her wish fulfilled. Jeremy never had any choice in her demands and decisions.

"That's the problem with Jeremy. He is only a good server and nothing more," she said as she drove home thereafter.

Even though Precious and Oko communicated on an average of two times a day, first thing in the morning, and the last thing before bed, they never set a date to meet. Both were living out the fantasies perceived in each other and for each other. As fate would have it, their face to face meeting wouldn't be long.

On a chilly January 9th, they met at the entrance to their school building. She looked at him and said, "Mr. Oko, how are you this cold day. I hope it was not too cold for you? I hope your trip went well? When did you arrive?" She seems nervous, evidenced by her rapid succession of questions.

"Thanks, Precious, and Happy New Year. By the way, you're beautiful as always," he replied.

"See you later," she said, as she walked away as if she cared less of seeing him. She was just playing the love game. She even refused to acknowledge his compliments. If the truth be told, she was at a crossroad. Even though they saw each other at least once a week in class, he was always afraid to request a face to face private meeting with her.

The sketches, letters, and cards continued. He was becoming restless and constantly formulating how to summon enough courage to approach her and ask for a date.

Precious, on the other hand, continued to suffer in silence. She had many wet nights and had woken up many mornings in cold sweats, wondering if she should call him. Then, it occurred to her that she didn't have his telephone number, even if she had wanted to.

Oko had had enough of his suffering. A few weeks later, he waited for her before class. When she arrived at the door leading to their department, he approached her and said, "Excuse me, Ms. Precious, I would like to speak with you after class, if you don't mind."

They hardly concentrated during the class period. All they did during the entire class session was doodle about each other. At the end of the class session, she was waiting for him in the hallway.

Oko gathered his things and rushed to see her. Before he could meet his precious queen, his professor asked him to come to his office to discuss his research internship. "Lord, why now," he said aloud. He forgot he had asked God in prayers for the internship but the love of his heart was now more important. Luckily for him, the Lord always understood that His children, on earth, only pray at their time of need and forgot about Him when the needs are met.

He quickly ran to her in the hallway and said, "I'm sorry I have to see professor Pendagratt for a second."

"That's ok. I'll wait for you in the school cafeteria."

"Today is my lucky day," Oko said to himself. After all, there was an African proverb that said, "With time, an egg will walk. With patience, I'll have her," he said to himself again as he ran to see his professor.

Precious sat gracefully at the cafeteria as he approached her as if he was summoned to the King's court to be made a Knight.

"Hello Precious. You look gorgeous" he told her again. "Thanks, you look handsome yourself," she replied.

"Can I order you anything?" he asked. "The food here is horrible. I'll have what you're having," she told him.

Oko ordered two catfish sandwiches with fat free mayonnaise, slices of tomatoes, onions, sliced eggs, cheese, turkey bacon, and fresh lettuce. For dessert, he ordered, two mugs of hot chocolate with whipped cream on top. He offered her a serving. "Thanks. This is my favorite," she commented.

"I know. You may be surprised how much I know about you." "You must be paying attention to my Facebook blog," she commented. "Yes, and much more," he replied.

She dips her finger in the whip cream and licked it while looking at him as if to be saying, "This is your dick, my love." He was clueless. He will learn sooner than later—welcome to America. Welcome to Precious' world.

They ate in silence and periodically looked at each other. Then, she broke the silence and said, "Mr. Oko, you said you wanted to tell me something, I'm here." She had jokes calling him Mr. to his face.

Oko smiled and said, "Thanks, Miss Precious." He then brought out twenty two cards and letters. One meant for everyday he was away in Ghana. He opened one of the cards and read it to her. It was another card by the American Greetings:

> *Since I met you, all I can think about is making you happy. I want to see your smile and hear your laughter. I want to kiss away old hurts and hold you until you know without a doubt that this is for real.*

> *I want to memorize the sound of your voice and the dreams of your heart . . . more than anytime else, I want to make you happier than you've ever been before and give you all the things that you truly deserve.*

Then, he opened one of his own letters:

> *I believe honesty is the single most important aspect of a lasting relationship. Therefore, I think there's something you should know . . . I honestly want to have sex with you right now.*

She looked around in case anyone within hearing distance was listening. She hushed him, and said, "Please, not here."

He smiled and replied, "I'll tell the world about how I feel about you."

She smiled again and said, "You're so crazy."

"Yes, I'm crazy alright. I'm crazy for you."

He laughed and continued to tell the reason for his request to meet with her. He wanted to let her know he's in love with her even if he wasn't sure the feeling was mutual.

"Ms. Precious, I'm glad you're able to meet me today. You know I had tried to approach you several times but I couldn't find the right time or moment. I wanted to know you more so that I don't come to you unprepared. I also know you have a boyfriend. I've weighed the consequences of my resolve; so far, I've no other choice but to tell you my feelings. I don't want to go through life thinking I had missed the chance to let you know how I feel about you. I love your beauty. I love the way you carry yourself. I love the way you make me feel from inside, just from my thought of you. I've attempted to show you my feelings, at least, in a limited way. Miss Precious, I want you to know me better. For your information, I have all the patience in the world. If I have the chance, I want to invite you to a movie or catch a play or walk in the park together. I want to extend an invitation to cook one of my country's cuisines for you. Please, accept. Here are my phone numbers. The second number is my cell. You can reach me anytime on either one."

She thanked him for his attention over the few months and confessed that she had felt bad that she couldn't connect with him before this time. She also confessed that she was attracted to him and would admit that she had wanted to stop him many times just to say hi. Then, she asked, "May I ask you one question? Be honest with me, please. Are you seeing or dating anyone right now?"

"Not at the moment," he replied.

Precious signaled to him that she has to leave for the next class. She stood up and thanked him for lunch and promised to think about everything.

She had not told him the real reason for rushing off. Oko knew there were no more classes in the entire school that day. It was the last day before mid-term break. She realized her lies on her way to her joint counseling session with her fiancé, Jeremy. In her state of mind, she cared less about the counseling and Jeremy. She had been with Jeremy so long the love between them was stale and taken for granted. The thrill was gone in the love they once shared. The length of time they lived together had accumulated in truck load the negative side of their relationship even if everything seemed hunky dory to the rest of the world.

In her mind, Precious would prefer to start anew with someone with less painful baggage. Someone she is certain may be going places. She was not looking for a perfect man but a man perfect for her. She wanted an individual who appreciates arts, nature, and culture. She preferred an individual who could mentally and physically challenge her. Most especially, someone with a foreign accent who could make her clit twinkle. Frankly speaking, she would prefer someone like Oko, if not him in the flesh. "Shit, I prefer and want O," she told herself silently as she drove to her counseling appointment. All wet . . . all horny as hell . . . Oko was the cause of her sexual dilemma.

After their session, Jeremy offered to take her to dinner at her favorite Mexican restaurant. At dinner, she could see Oko's sexy images flashing in front of her. She was now emotionally detached from Jeremy's affections. Except for the obligatory sex encounters she demanded from him, she was done with him for all practical purposes. The comfortable and family oriented aspects of their relationship were in the toilet, to say the least.

The confession of Oko of his love interest had made anything but easy. It wasn't the best day for therapy. Frankly, she didn't give a damn any longer about the counseling and/or Jeremy. She had just justified sleeping with Oko as rational—the beginning of the end for Jeremy.

CHAPTER 11

Precious didn't attend classes the week following the mid-term break. She hadn't called Oko either. He missed her terribly and was worried of what might have happened to his love. He could only message her on Facebook. He did. She replied and told him she was not feeling well and above all, she wasn't ready to listen to Professor Lamberk's boring logic and ethics class. She would've preferred to attend instead, a class in the future official language of America: Spanish.

Oko immediately sent her a dozen roses with a get well card. He would have taken the flowers to her in person but he couldn't make the 150 miles round trip with his 1991 Pontiac he just bought for five hundred dollars, from a seventy-nine year old member of his church. It seemed love had its limit . . . What's more, his action may be considered pushy and invasive. Her fiancé, Jeremy, was another factor—with everyone's right to bear arms and stand their grounds, he didn't want to risk it.

Even if she wanted to date Oko on the side, the 150 miles round trip had not made it appetizing, especially when she was horny late nights and wanted a booty call on demand. Precious contemplated, in her mind, the possibility of making the long distance drive to see Oko while still sleeping with her fiancé, Jeremy. She just wasn't sure how to incorporate one love affair into the mix.

"A periodic escape to Richmond may be what my pussy ordered," she tried to convince herself.

With her favorite white wine, she sat down to read the latest issue of Africa and Beyond Magazine. The feature article was, "America, I'm grateful," written by Oko Nyembe N. Kediri, a Master's degree candidate.

CHAPTER 12

America, I Am Grateful.
By
Oko N. Kediri, Graduate Student.
Concentration: Economics of Christian religion.

September 6, 2011 marked the fourth year since my arrival to this great country, on a jet plane. It is befitting to take a few minutes to express my gratitude to a nation that, in many ways, has made many of my dreams come true.

I remember, like yesterday, the tedious process of obtaining a passport. But all the hard work and obstacles were quickly forgotten when my visiting visa was granted at exactly 10:14am after my second attempts.

I still remember the embassy's personnel on their way to their offices, picking up litters left behind by some visa applicants on their perfectly manicured lawn. There and then, they had sold me their country forever.

I vividly remember the marines on duty, in their elegant and professional uniforms, and by so doing made their country proud.

I can still hear the voice of the gentleman who handed me my visa, saying, "Mr. Kediri, welcome to the United States of America." Yes, he called me "Mr."

To me, they were all ambassadors of their country: the country of Jefferson, Lincoln, Martin Luther King, and the main man, Barack Obama.

Upon returning to my little Okungbowa village with my fresh minted visiting visa, my friends, well-wishers, and even foes alike, rejoiced, and celebrated with me. They came with original palm wine and plenty of beer for the so called "Been-tos"—those who can no longer drink our local "Oguro" (palm wine) because they had travelled abroad, in white man's land, and found local wine unpalatable and unbecoming of someone with overseas travel experiences.

My mother graced the occasion with her original pounded yam, special finger licking egusi soup, cooked with slightly salted organic goat meat, cow legs, crayfish, onions, red pepper, fresh tomatoes, canned tomato, her secret herbs, and green vegetables, all smothered in palm oil.

Every invitee to the festivity prayed to the Deity with kola-nuts and bitter kolas, as they poured libation to our ancestors for my safety to the foreign land, my safe return, and prosperity. What a feast I had.

On my departing day, I couldn't wait to reach my destination. I was looking forward to the 12-hour flight, courtesy of Delta Airways.

I remember waving farewell to my mother, wife, children, and close friends. I left behind my pains and occasional joy.

I was looking forward to all I ever dreamed about in a promised land. The land I had seen through the eyes of those who went before me or from the words of those who never saw it but professed to know all about it.

I wanted to see for myself the people whose voices came through so clearly on the Voice of America at 2:00am daily, from my brother's Telefunken radiogram.

I couldn't wait to see the cities as seen in the movies where I thought, "I don't have to do much to have everything in a foreign land." Even today, many from the motherland still believe money grows on trees or lining the streets of the Unites States of America from Key West to Anchorage, Alaska. I wish the heavens could open up so that they can see for themselves all about America. Regrettably, I doubt that ever happening. Oops, I forgot Google maps . . .

I couldn't wait to see live, the great musicians. I wanted to meet the movie stars in person as they appeared on film projectors shown by foreign marketing entities, in my village motor park, selling their foreign products. Pepsodent toothpaste was one of them. Ever since the introduction of their product, the native's chewing stick, containing herbs and other natural ingredients, to clean our teeth was out, modern toothpaste was in.

I wanted to meet the beautiful black Americans and their big afros, especially the Queen of Soul, Aretha Franklin. I wished one day, I would be blessed to see the greats—Chaka khan, Mohamed Ali, Prince, Beyonce, The Staple Singers, James Brown, and the man who sang "Return to Sender," Elvis Presley.

I had dreamt of seeing "live" Isaac Hayes, and the best Jazz aficionado, Blues Boy—B.B. King and his beloved, Lucile. I wanted to see with my own eyes Marvin Gaye, Earth Wind and Fire, and The Temptations, instead of listening to their voices on my 33" albums played with my ten-year old turn table, a gift from my brother.

I wanted to see Ray Charles, Barry White (with his 54-member Orchestra), and Frankie Beverly on stage at the coliseum. Yes, I wanted to see the fabulous Rick James, and KC and the Sunshine Band too. Have I mentioned, MJ, the man that gave us Billie Jean, Michael Jackson? I especially prayed to see him live, on stage . . .

I wanted to sojourn in the land where movie star greats: Sidney Poitier, Earl Jones, Morgan Freeman, Dorothy Dandridge, Rubby Dee, Cecily Tyson, La Wanda page, Lena Horne, Hatti McDaniel, the funny man, Bill Cosby, and the chairman of the board himself, Frank Sinatra, to mention just a few.

Many have passed on now, but I still have their memories. They were all blessed Americans.

To me and all my friends back home, these music and movie legends were presumed to be living large in big houses, in the same neighborhood, and driving pleasure cars in God's own country. They were considered the pride of America everywhere.

I came and saw the glitters, the sky scrapers of New York, the good roads (smooth and wide, without potholes), 24-hour running water, indoor plumbing and toilets with clean water, clear and looking good enough to drink. Yes, I said it, if the truth be told.

TV was at my command with remote control. I wasted many valuable hours surfing all available channels without purpose. I listened to all the black radio stations and said to myself; blacks are beautiful people. To me, everything was just beautiful!

I registered for my classes and anxious to become all I wanted to be and more.

I graduated from college in three years without bribing any school officials. My college mentors admired my ability. They fine-tuned my potentials and shared their wisdom without tribal affiliations.

I was allowed the freedom to pursue any discipline of my choice. They made learning so easy and challenging. They all seem to love what they do. No teachers' strike like schools in my native land. One of my teachers once told me, "We couldn't strike because we have contracts and wanted better future for the students and our country."

As a full-time college student, I worked part-time, an average of 39.50 hours a week on campus earning $5.10 per hour, before taxes, of the American's almighty dollars. There and then, I knew the American God truly existed as I dreamt it.

With my master's degree in a few months, I must say now that this country, this United States of America, gave me life. Maybe, I should accurately say, my third life. My mother and father gave me the first. They did their best with relentless love they knew how. I almost surrendered that life to my maker at the age of nine, the first of my three attempts.

My maternal grandparents gave me the second life. They trained and raised me with all the morals they possessed. They taught me to respect others, to work hard or harder if I must (oh yes, I did plenty of that). They pounded in my head, in my native language, whether I liked it or not, words like endurance, respect, honesty, determination, and perseverance. I can still remember my grandfather's father-to-son constant and the daily talk about life, and my responsibilities to it.

I'm grateful, grandparents. I pray your souls continue to rest in perfect peace as you continue to rest on the right hand of the Lord, our redeemer.

I acquired my own stereo system with CD player, when less than ten years earlier, I wasn't even allowed to touch the knob of a transistor radio because my kind in the family was not eligible to do so. Yes, prejudice and discrimination exist in my family too. The same way it exists in the continent of Africa. The same way it exists in this great land I'm falling in love with so much.

Yes, I do experience discrimination and prejudices. Such ignorance of the people, by the people, to the people, would not deter my endeavor to succeed and be somebody. After all, there is no cure for such mentality, everywhere.

I was able to rent my own furnished one bedroom apartment equipped with kitchen, living room, and dinette. All mine, all within the walls of my abode. I am now the man as I was meant to be by my God Almighty. Yes, my own God Almighty . . .

All things considered, no one can convince me otherwise that this is not the greatest country on earth. To me and my house, United States of America "Is it."

Sadly enough however, I cannot comprehend the actions of American men, women, young, and old alike, who on a daily basis are not taking advantage of all the great opportunities available to them in this great country. A country, with hard work, anyone can "Be all you can be" like its Army slogan before they changed it to "Army of one." I love the old slogan better, though.

I saw homeless people and street beggars on the streets of America cities just like my native land. I visited Harlem and the east side of the windy city, Chicago, and saw the decays and rundown neighborhoods. I saw the pictures and TV documentaries of the tragedy in Katrina. For a brief moment, I thought I was seeing documentary about the slums of Lagos, Nigeria or the dirty beaches of Togo or the South Africa Townships or Peckham in London. It seems, the more different countries are far apart, the more they are the same. I love it all.

My heart aches when I see children disrespecting themselves, their parents, their elders, and anyone else they intend to disrespect for all reasons. I see the same group of people, who were disrespected, disrespecting their children and everybody else. I see parents incapable of raising their children on basic life responsibilities and expectations—humbleness, honesty, appreciation, consideration, and how to say simple thank you. I see husbands disrespecting their wives and wives disrespecting their husbands. I see boyfriends disrespecting their girlfriends and girlfriends disrespecting their boyfriend, and so on . . . all in the name of the American way and freedom of speech. But again, these basic functions have now been left to television personalities. I saw one TV personality, joking and laughing while telling his co-hosts that the room of his six-year old is always like a tornado passed through it—he was proud of it too.

I just cannot understand the high rate of school dropouts in light of all the opportunities awaiting them with good education or any education for that matter, when many children around the world pray to the same American God for a taste of the American blessings and grace. These unfortunate and neglected children all over the world are just asking their own governments for a fraction of what ordinary Americans are blessed with and constantly taken for granted. Ironically, the same foreign leaders come to America to spend their ill-gotten money as millions of their citizens suffer on a daily basis and when their citizens turned against them, by any means, they seek the assistance of their godfathers . . . I love America for ignoring the pains of the oppressed around the world, under the hegemony of the blessed supreme five at the United Nations—the world organization of political parties. And when the people take up arms to demand better standard of living, America then evokes "National interest" so as to maintain autocratic democracy. Many are killed because few had been chosen . . .

I just don't get it anymore when many don't want to work hard or add value to their lives or aspire to be somebody. Negativism and never ending complaints have now replaced ambition, self-development, and empowerment. Majority of the citizens now blame their presidents if the sky is blue at dusk or the private plane landing is rough in Anchorage, Alaska instead of the same rough landing in Kalamazoo as predicted by the experts on their website, www. landinginkalamazooinerror.com

It amazes me when people of all ages are in the business of crimes, hatred, discrimination, senseless killings of innocent citizens including women and children.

Many partake in get-rich quick schemes because they must have the latest of everything. To them, all that glitters must be gold, the same ideology embraced by my people, in my country and environs. I can now declare that we are all God's children anywhere in the world. I love it.

I watch with agony the continued erosion or the loss of many African American's economic freedom in spite of their enormous economic purchasing power running into billions of dollars, far more than the annual budgets of dozens of countries in continental Africa without natural resources. I love it when I realized African Americans are ignorant of these facts . . .

I still do not understand why many in our midst want to blame others for all their shortcomings, without a little effort of their own. I wish they engage their mirrors and see the inadequacies in themselves. Better yet, let them clear the specks in their own eyes.

What's more, American leaders, many in politics and some as agents of God, joined in the same misdirection for their own personal agenda—they say what their constituents want them to say or hear. They continue to ignore the obvious. They must be politically correct, lest, their reelection or ability to remain in power of authority fall in peril. Many of them worked so hard to keep the job they hated and constantly criticized.

I find it difficult when American top leaders play macho with the rest of the world in light of the fact that those they speak to with chosen name calling really admire them. The people of these countries are not jealous of what Americans have; rather, they just want America to show fairness in their leadership to the world as endowed upon us by the Almighty. Maybe, fairness is not an operative word anymore, I'm convinced fairness and understanding will go a long way to improve relationships in the world, for the benefits of all God's children. American leaders can do more than what they are doing now. "Yes, they can."

I found peace within myself, when I read that in America, government performed illegal medical experiments on its citizens, the same way, African governments are doing with their own people, many times, aided and abetted by foreign governments or entities.

To me, I know the American dream is well and alive. I just don't think many of its citizens are doing enough to take advantage of it.

At this juncture, I must ask, "By whose authority do these leaders and the citizens do these things?" As I see it, Jesus Christ died for the multitude. It is about time we made Him proud for His sacrifices. Frankly, I'm of the opinion, it's too late.

I'll say no more on this subject because I ought to leave the preaching of His words to the chosen few. Bishop T D Jakes, Pastor Matthew Warren, and Pastor Joe Olsten, please, don't forget us in your prayers.

Of course, I'm not saying that my life is full of roses in this United States. I've my own share of tears, pains, and the "Why me" questions I always ask myself during tough times in my journey so far.

To this end, my message here is to put aside my bad experiences and recount the blessings and opportunities accorded me by this beautiful country and its great people.

After all, I don't want to give another life to the period somewhere in Norfolk, as a dishwasher where many of my kind couldn't enter the dining area of a private club because of our dark skin. The light-skin amongst us got a little break of busting tables and serving the club members. I even love this scenario because I was reliving the days when my country was under the colonial masters—same difference.

Yes, many of my kind entered and left through the back door to pick up their paychecks. But, I really don't have any right to complain because the same discrimination happened to me and my kind in my own family, in my own country, back home. I just wasn't expecting it in God's own country.

Today, however, with my greenbacks and/or credit/ debit cards in my pocket, I can eat practically anywhere I want to. Ok, maybe I'm going too far with the eating anywhere part.

Looking back now, I'm determined more than ever to establish my own private club with membership made up of loving people everywhere. I want a club where anyone, regardless of color, race, religious background, sexual preferences, and country of origin, can enter and leave as they wish, and making the American dollars in the process.

What is America to me?

It's a country of contrasts.

America is a country where, children are paid or bribed to clean their rooms or for getting better grades in school, and later in life, the same folks championing such behavior, some of them from Ivy League researchers, complained that the same children are lazy, irresponsible, ungrateful, unappreciative, and selfish.

It's a country where minority leaders—parents, politicians, educators, professionals, and anyone with microphones blame one hundred percent of minority's problems on the majority—white people, rich people, and powerful people; the same way the leaders in my native land blame foreign governments for all their country's woes. I love the similarity of human race, everywhere.

It's a country where few continue to do the right things and many refused to comprehend the rights thing to do, at any age. What a country of unconscious diversity . . . I love it.

It's a great country where its laws, supported by the judicial system, aided and abetted divorces, encourages excessive child support payments, and avoids adjudicating equal responsibilities to parents for bringing a child to the world. Later in life, the same court system and its citizens blamed dysfunctional families mostly on single parenting and the lack or inadequate welfare support. Oh Lord, America is beautiful for all its flaws.

It's a country where citizens call the emergency number (911) because their cable TV wasn't working during their Monday night football.

Shit, pardon my foul language—I'm just fed up a little because it's a country where people in power still blame their own government as a way of attaining their agenda.

It's a country where anyone can say any shit under the freedom of expression. In less than four years, I'm pleased to say, with pride, that I'm mastering the

American English language—shit, fuck, mother-fucker, son-of-a-bitch, asshole, to name just a few. What's more, many in my native land already added such international style of expressions in their vocabulary. With such American language under my belt, I'm confident I'll pass my citizen's test when the time comes. I can now say it like many before me, "If you don't like the American ways, then, get the fuck out."

It's a country where social lingos are creeping into the English dictionary. The word, "Like" is now in every spoken sentence by their citizens under thirty years of age. God, I love the Kardashians, the Bad Girls Club, the Meet the Browns, and many media programs educating us and the next generations everything despicable about life: laziness, rudeness, disrespect, verbal abuse, vulgarity, violence, and you name it. Many of us are getting fucked everyday with pride, still smiling, and refused to acknowledge anything, howbeit perished. I love America and how they cover all aspects of life.

It's a country where anyone with money, connections, and expensive lawyers, can ascertain that their clients get away with anything. In America, the innocents are arrested, read their rights, and provided with lawyers if they can't afford one, with all the arsenal of the rule of law at their disposal. After trial, they are still sentenced to death or something close to it. In my native land, on the other hand, the innocents are arrested, tried in kangaroo court, and timely sentenced to death without the rule of law—in the end, the same cup of tea, in both God's land. I love it.

It's a country where many enrich themselves heartlessly and live lavishly by maximizing price and profit from banking, real estate, retail, technology, energy, entertainment, hospitality, etc. In the end, however, these oligarchies gave away some on their windfall for charitable causes. Some of their good deeds are happening in Africa—in education, feeding the hungry, politics, and health care. In my native land, on the other hand, many with similar opportunities enriched themselves, by any means necessary. Then, their ill-gotten gains or loots, to be blunt, from their citizens and the national resources of all citizens are used exclusively for their own personal wealth and enjoyment, all of the time—big houses, fleet of automobiles, showering their wives and girlfriends with anything money can buy under the sun, sending their children to the best schools at home and abroad, accumulating harem of women, vacationing abroad, and investing the remaining wealth overseas. These leaders don't give a shit about the rest of their people—pardon my language, I'm just fed up. The irony of it all is that many preach and want us to believe there is no heaven on hearth. I love some Americans and their creed. I equally love the people of my native land for doing the same and getting better at it than the Americans who drafted the blueprint.

It's a country where many that killed and/or abuse drugs, later became TV stars and talk show darlings after rehabilitations and/or upon completing their jail terms. They subsequently write books about their journey to-date, go on a lecture circuit, and become heroes to many. I love America, the land of opportunity, regardless of how defined.

It's a country where so-called experts agreed that all politics are local but the same pundits refused to see the consequences of that philosophy on issues affecting the nation as a whole. It's happening right now in American national politics—it's called Obama by any other name . . . .

It's a country where many people, especially those morally associated with religious empire, are allowed to read books according to their gospels, and in the end, many become mediocre in their exposure to diverse knowledge.

It's a country where many children and students, expected to be leaders of tomorrow, are not allowed to read books on evolution, the environment, and other related books. As a result, they lack the capability to tackle the ever changing challenges of today and future years. On the other hand, foreign students who are free to study sciences and technology, will ultimately fill the jobs where Americans are no longer able to compete. I may be overreaching, but nearly all science, technology, and engineering departments, in many high schools and post-secondary educational institutions, are overpopulated by foreign trained and/or foreign born teachers and students. I love America even more for the opportunities accorded future immigrants as a result of the shallow minds of their leaders and those that made them leaders.

It's a country where many refused to go to school, and those that attend schools, dropped out for all sort of reasons. And those that stayed in schools don't want to study. Those that studied pursue disciplines of no economic value—still burdened with tuition or education related debts. In the end, the same students and the supporters of their lazy ass complained how they can't find decent good paying jobs. The country's solution: hire foreign workers to fill the good paying jobs. I love the derived opportunities available to foreign citizens. I really want to rewrite the famous words of Paul Revere, "The British are coming," and say, the foreigners are here, the foreigner will be coming . . .

It's a country where many who never planned or save for retirement, later complained they can't sustain their old age and life style on social security benefits alone. Just as in my native land, it's all excuses upon excuses. Each day, I am feeling at home here because I can see the faces of my own people on American faces.

It's a country where the poor make the rich richer by consuming everything in their dreams produced and sold to them by the rich or rich entities, including anything fake, even when they couldn't afford them financially or emotionally. They find a way to buy two hundred dollar celebrity snickers, T-shirts, jackets, and you name it for themselves and their children but couldn't afford to buy school supplies for the same children—such important school supplies and clothing are left to charitable organization. I observe folk with minimum wages buying specialized coffee from the popular franchised coffee houses—where they call each customer by name. In the end, seek sympathy from the heavens, with prayers when they can't pay their utility bills. They forget the scripture, according to the book of Matthew 25:29, "For everyone who has, more shall be given, and he will have abundance, but from the one who does not have, even what he does have shall be taken away." The poor people in America know how to make the rich richer just like the poor people in my native land. I love the mental equality, to some extent, of all people everywhere.

It's a country where politicians talk to each other instead of with each other when it comes to any issues. It's becoming a taboo for politicians from opposing parties to agree on anything. They have one good attribute; however, they fight for some of their constituents' issues and personal agenda, most of the time. Conversely, in my native land, politicians only disagree when it affects their personal allotment of the national cake—nothing else matters. I love the children of God and their selfish greed, anywhere.

It's a country where some will despise you and many others will adore you.

It's a country where anyone has the choice to fail and plenty of opportunities to succeed.

It's a country where many acquire wealth like there is no tomorrow but layoff their workforce to cut costs and boost their bottom line in other to achieve higher returns on their investments. I understand their plights, however.

It's a country with endless land of opportunities but homelessness is growing, and many children go hungry each night.

It's a country where mismanagement of the environment is always a subject for debate regardless of the negative consequences on future generations. I love it. I love it because in my native land, there is no such debate because pollution and the destruction of the environment are our ways of life. We don't give a fuck about such matters. People of my native land should feel vindicated because many Americans don't give a shit either.

Lest I forget, unlike in my native land where public universities are closed at will because government leaders-in-charge woke up on the wrong side of the bed; American leaders shutdown their government because the party occupying the American house, is unacceptable to the party that lost the election bout. I love it all because we are no longer judged by the color of our skin but by the ideology the few must protect.

It's a country of love and made for lovers.

It's a country with plenty of national parks and monuments for its citizens to admire, love, enjoy, and preserved for future generations, the way their founding fathers intended. My goodness, America is beautiful.

It's a country of pro-life folks but the same group is willing to kill those that disagree with their agenda, and/or defund any assistance for the living. I love America even with their chameleon expressions.

It's a country advocating for peace and yet managed multi-billion dollar war machine in the name of world peace and territorial integrity. I do sympathize with the reason or reasons America does what it does because to do otherwise will make her uncompetitive among nations of the world with the same agenda.

It's a country with the right to bear arms by anyone who can pull a trigger and when the innocent are killed, everyone gathered, prayed, make political speeches for and against the person or persons that caused the atrocity, and then call it a day, until the next mass killings.

It's a country advocating justice, openness, fairness, and yet, turns blind eyes to atrocities all over the world for lack of national interest.

It's a country with their own brand of corruptions, which I can best describe as good corruptions. A country that turned blind eyes to structural corruption in many developing countries under what they described as "Contained diplomacy." I call such ingenious strategy for another land, bad corruption.

It's a country where health care for all is subject to debates, all in the name of money and political differences. Oh Lord, please help America so that they can in turn help the people of my native land because my God knows that the people of my native land can't help themselves.

It's a country where few farmers and agribusinesses are feeding many all over the world without much fanfare but Brittney Spears, the super star, is celebrated for shaving her head.

It's a country where anyone who can make noises on the airwaves is considered analyst and/or expert and in so doing, can dispense free advice to those who refused to think for themselves. It seems diverse reading and learning that used to energize the mind, is now going the way of dinosaur. Passive accumulation of knowledge is now the norm of the society. Television and cable programs are now the original sources of knowledge and wisdom. That's cool, America . . .

It's a country where the President carries his own briefcase. As an African born, I couldn't comprehend that one. Americans have no respect for their leaders and elders. I'm sure I may be missing something . . .

It's a country where congressman and women, reporters, and self-proclaimed advocate of freedom of expressions shout at and on the president of the United States, the most powerful man on earth. I'm sure they have reasons for doing what they do. Their disrespect for the office of the Presidency still doesn't make any sense to me, regardless of the freedom of speech they claimed, by the constitution, as their divined authority. What an irony, the same disrespectful folks are convincing their followers and admirers how well they are raising their own children to be exemplary leaders of tomorrow. They may have a point though; after all, I'm still a new comer to this great land.

It's a country where women and/or blacks running for the office of the presidency must still subscribe to the identity litmus test even though they are leaders, mothers, and fathers in their own rights. One of them is still defending the legitimacy of his election to the highest office in the land. What an irony—this great country can still look Jesus Christ, the son of God in the face, and consciously tell other nations the spirit of democracy and how to practice it.

Only in America is where everyone is encouraged to be what they want to be, but their character, gender, and race, will be scrutinized senselessly when they try to be what they are encouraged to be.

It's a country where many women champion their independence, creativity, and intelligence but complained adamantly that they can't raise or control their children by themselves without the assistance of a man. Are these women saying, they can't raise their children alone after they claimed they are all that? These women and their advocate believe two heads are better than one, even though, one of the heads may be rotten to the core. At times, it seems, both heads are now rotten to the bone . . .

Yes, I love the way many Americans see things in black and white when it comes to matters of national interest and in rainbow colors when it comes to the rest of the world. Their school of thought reminded me of the citizens of my native land—always adamant to unproductive tradition, beliefs, and culture. Heavens, I feel at home already in America.

It's a country where women or men knowingly slept or do whatever, with married public figures, then sprint to the tabloids and television producers to tell their country men and women all about the affairs. Yet, no one challenges their culpability in the whole matter. All the media want out of the deal is fresh-dripping-blood, ratings, and destruction of the accused, regardless of any other goodness possessed by the accused. America has now added sex and video tape to money as the roots of all evil. I love such mentality because I'm already used to short sightedness of a nation before my arrival.

It's a country where parents must obtain permission to talk to their two-year olds and later wonder why the same child at seven, behave badly and do bad things behind closed doors. The same children later in life blame their parents for their life shortcomings because they too lack the ability to look into their souls and see where they took the wrong turn in life. No one ever taught them how. They never taught themselves how . . .

It's a country where energy companies must maximize profits for their investors. The same investors, after consuming the same energy company's products, later complained about high energy prices. Now, I ask, how in sweet God's name can the two goals complement each other? Definitely, I am falling in love with the greed of American capitalism because when I've some money, I too will invest in such entities for my retirement.

It's a country deep rooted in democracy with individual freedom and liberty for all, but some are condemned for their sexual orientation and religious beliefs—the same fundamental values once held so dearly in 1776 manifesto, are no longer relevant when valued positions collide with politics or political parties. I love America for their selfish and naïve mentality. I love it because I can relate perfectly before this homecoming . . .

It's a country with freedom of religion but on the pulpit, religious leaders point fingers at each other and condemned other religion as ungodly and evil. Each brand of religion sanctions only their own brand for all, as the only path to the Kingdom of Heaven. Each sect wants their own God as the only God for all. America, I love your religious' modus operandi even when such religious school of thought of one shoe fits all, may be irrational and illogical. Ironically, I was taught or I might have read somewhere that the original immigrants left Europe to the new world for freedom of religion—I plan to read over the American history one more time, in case, I've missed something. I must have . . .

It's a country where religious purist preached against reading Harry Potter series or any other related books except their one and only Book, but celebrated Halloween with their children. But again, this annual celebration is big business and good for the economy. I love America and their different standards for convenience.

It's a country full of hopes and opportunities. It's a country where many people, including teachers, parents, school children, politicians, business owners, religious leaders, entertainers, and many more, fight for the common man, woman, and children. I like these aspects of America too.

It's a country where obesity is openly criticized but junk foods are sold everywhere directly to children and their food addicted weak-minded parents, guardians, and relatives. I love how the American companies resolve to conquer and destroy their future consumers and the environment—all in the name of money, oh Lord.

It's a country where citizens grow up consuming unhealthy foods, polluted their body with additives, consumed illegal substances, and later complained of high medical costs of curing the diseases resulted from their lifestyle. It's a society where almost all functions are operated by remote controls, and later complained of couch potato persons. I'm guilty too because I just bought a "Clap-Off" recently to turn off my bedside lamp—maybe one can attribute this ways of life to the price of civilization and therefore ok. After all, in my native land, especially in many villages, poor people (most of them are) enjoyed the benefits of their poverty—they eat plenty of fresh food without chemicals: vegetables, mushrooms, naturally raised cows, chickens, goats, more vegetable, more mushrooms, and drink fresh water. I'm in America now and all that good shit is no longer part of my diet . . . sweet . . .

There is good news America! As a result of these inadequate behaviors, habits, and ideologies, multi-billion dollar companies came alive to cure the same problems for tidy profit. When all is said and done, jobs are created, economy is expanding. I really wish African countries and their leaders take a page from the American's economic strategic plans, if they are truthful in expanding their economies; after all, what's good for the soul may not necessarily be good for the economy or vice versa. It seems the more I run away from my native land; the more I'm reliving it. I love it.

I'm used to the American discrimination and racism because in my native land, their brand of the same inhuman ideology is called tribalism or nepotism. We are not too far apart even when we are thousands of miles apart. Thank you, dear Jesus, for blessing most of us with the same mentality, everywhere. I shouldn't be surprised, however, because my Bible tells me we can all trace our roots to the first grandparents, Adam and Eve.

I love and envy America for its freedom of speech in any fashion. Many of its citizens, taking such freedom to the extreme, may be another matter.

I admire the American's violent movies and pornographic films produced in Hollywood and elsewhere, all in the name of freedom of speech and expression. It's comical to me when in the end; its citizens complain about violent behavior among the citizenry who no longer value human life—everyone wants to grow up and be just like those good guys from the Sopranos, The Godfather, Scarface, National Born killer, and so forth. Cool . . .

I love the sitcoms on television where actors and actresses insult and disrespect their elders, promote laziness, and celebrate irresponsibility. Their jokes degrade anyone working in fast food establishments or any low paying jobs. Subsequently, everyone complains about their citizens expecting more for nothing. Individual responsibility to walk before they can run is now a dying philosophy. To me, these jokers are by no means funny. And they wander why another twenty millions may be coming, across the border from the west, in another fifteen years? Please, who among us is willing to do their jobs?

I love the high spirit in every American. Ok, let me be clearer, I love the spirit in most Americans. I love their ethnocentrism—where what is good for America is good for the world just like its baseball, played by Americans, on American soil, and yet, they call it the 'World Series.' I love such pride and prejudice in American souls. Unlike folks in my native land, there is no such national pride or spirit. To most of my people, everything foreign is worshiped—especially imported goods from America but made in China or somewhere else. Their own products are inferior or valueless, except their natural resources, limited brain drains, and cultural dancers. Lord, forgive me; I almost forgot the animal kingdoms . . .

America has them all: the good, the bad, and the unexplained. Only in America can they all coexist beautifully. To me, America is the greatest.

Today, I walk tall with pride when I visit my country of birth. I'm sure many in my village are now admiring me for all they want to make of me. Many want their children to be like me without adequate evaluation of my status quo. Many family members who once wrote my obituary before my death are now extending their good wishes and selected respect, still for a price. Many demand rewards even when they had not contributed to my survival or existence—I was once their houseboy or house help. In a way, I'm slowly winning my battle. America made that possible.

Ok, I realize I didn't participate in the struggles with the millions who fought and died for the freedom I now enjoy (no matter how limited that freedom is lately), my goal now is to make them proud of me so that they would know their efforts and sacrifices didn't go in vain.

This country had welcomed me with open arms—a country made of immigrants. Yes, I will repeat it; it's a country of immigrants. I'm one of the immigrants.

Ladies and gentlemen, I salute all the men and women who paved the way before me especially those in uniforms, who on a daily basis, continue to protect the freedom I now enjoy here at home and abroad.

I tip my hat to my college professors who guided me in my studies. I raise my hat to my new American friends who invited me to their homes and their many events to show me their American ways: how to walk like Americans, talk like Americans, cook like Americans, think like Americans, date their women like Americans, kiss like Americans, and even make love like Americans.

Just the other day, I witnessed a fellow who just came from Nigeria less than six weeks earlier and is now talking with American phonetics. Wow, I said. Then, I smiled because I know the power of American is in the air inhaled by all humans, everywhere.

I love American's ethnocentrism. I love it even when I am losing my identity or at least diluting it with my full knowledge that this society I'm in love with is decaying morally.

I must recognize countless others who, amidst all odds, stood by me at my most difficult times.

Of course, I must thank the Native Americans who first cultivated and blessed this homeland.

I'm grateful to the fathers of the Constitution. I must pay homage to the signers of 'American birth certificate,' the Declaration of Independence, where they declared that all men are created equal—the government of the people, by the people and for the people. I'm one of those men who were created equal. Their Constitution was written for me and my kind. To all of them, I simply say thank you.

If I've forgotten anyone, I forever beg for forgiveness. I'm grateful America. Yes, let me say it again, viva America!

September 25, 2012

CHAPTER 13

The more Precious read Oko's piece, the more she wanted him. The emotions in his article overwhelmed her. His appreciation of a country that accommodates him, to-date, made her shivers from within. His recognition that his people could or should empower themselves instead of blaming the rest of the world brought tears to her eyes. The fact that a foreign born admired the country she took for granted, some of the time, made her want to say aloud, like him, "America, I'm grateful."

She took another sip of her wine and dialed Oko for the first time. As luck would have it, she could only leave a message. "Please, call me as soon as you get home," she pleaded.

She was about to turn in for the night when her phone rang. It was Oko. "Good evening, Ms. Precious," he greeted her.

"Evening, Mr. Oko. I just want to congratulate you on your article. It was a great and emotional piece," she commented in her sexiest but natural voice.

"Thanks Ms. Precious. It's great to hear your voice. I'm so glad you enjoyed it."

Unexpectedly, she wanted to know when he would cook the Ghanaian delicacy he promised.

"Would tomorrow, Friday, be too soon?"

"I don't mind but that would be a long drive for such a short notice," she said.

"Ms. Precious, if you don't mind, I will come down and pick you up for a seven o'clock dinner and bring you back in case you insist on the bring you back part'" Oko softly said with a smile.

"Ok, Mr. Oko. You've got a date, provided you bring me back as promised."

Precious loved how the evening ended. She loved the way Oko took charge with grace, energy, and sacrifice. In her mind, it was about time to have someone who knew what she wanted. Someone who would treat her like the woman she is and more. She was tired of being the man in a relationship. She adored someone smart, creative, romantic, and of course, someone with the potential ability to be sexually satisfying.

In her gut, Precious was certain Oko would definitely meet her sexually satisfying part. She knew she was seeing her promised land on the horizon: tomorrow.

She fell asleep a happy woman for the first time in months.

Even though Oko had been in the country for nearly four years, he was still culturally, emotionally, and physically different from any of the men she had dated in recent past.

While Oko was away, he had written her the most beautiful messages on her Facebook, professing how much he missed and loved her. Now that he had just returned from a month-long hiatus in his home country, she recounted his Facebook messages and sketches of her. Very soon, every ounce of her dream will be for real.

The sight of him, the first time they met, made her hands moist and her lips longing for his kisses. She wouldn't say Oko was exceptionally handsome; there was something about his physique that made him simply beautiful.

Maybe, it was his full lips. Maybe, it was his height. Maybe, it was the way he walked. Maybe, it was her thought of how he would perform with his rod inside her, or maybe, he was simply the purest red blooded and undiluted black African alive . . . To her, he is the man of her choice. With a slight thought of him, her pussy became wet and longing more of him.

Within minutes, she was in another world she had lived many nights before tonight. She was in jubilation once again. She celebrated Mr. Jessie Jackson's famous slogan, "Keep hope alive."

It was almost midnight. Precious was unable to sleep. She had a glass of water, a slice of cheese and crackers while flipping through the cable channels, hoping to catch some sleep in the process. She was still unable to sleep. She wasn't the type that took sleeping pills but this night; she wished she had developed that habit. Her sleeping pill has always been a perfect rod in her holes . . .

The thought of Oko contributed to her sleeplessness. The disdain she had for Jeremy was another factor—the one factor in her life she would like to put on hold forever. She was lonely even if she could get to her fiancé, Jeremy, within fifteen minutes, anytime she wished.

When Jeremy used to lie besides her in bed, the thought of Oko came to her mind over and over again. She wished Oko was the flesh besides her. She knew she had found true love in Okoism. She just knew it . . .

And better yet, she wanted to go to him and be in his bed if only for companionship in her lonely nights. Great sex always put her to sleep. It has always been her sleeping pill. And from now on, she wanted Oko's great sex, to be her sleeping pill.

Jeremy may be real; she was oblivious to his existence.

As she closed her eyes, she was cold all over, the same way she had always been when she was horny and wanted to be loved. She found herself rubbing gently her hard nipples the way she always did each morning when admiring her own beauty when putting on her clothes.

Precious slowly stood and walked to her daughter's former bedroom, locked the door, and curdled up with her favorite Italian-made white and black stripped elephant patterned pillows. She wanted to be in her daughter's room because the thought of fantasizing love making with another man while lying in the same bed she shared with her fiancé, Jeremy, would be tantamount to cheating. To-date, she had struggled to have a conscience, no matter how limited.

Lately, she wanted to be alone so that she could concentrate on Oko and his fine self. The thoughts of Oko continued to run through her mind as she lay in bed listening to the best of Coltrane . . . All she wanted to do was make love to him or vice versa. Her clit was erect and throbbing. She placed her right middle finger over her clit and tightly squeezed her thighs for maximum friction. Within minutes, her clit, with the right friction, would have started a bon fire for the Scouts.

The thought of calling Oko came to her. She dismissed the idea. She doesn't know him that well—close or personal. All Precious could do was curled up and pretended to go to sleep. She left her middle fingers in her pussy and drifted to sleep.

Within minutes, she found herself dialing Oko. He was unable to sleep as well. He picked up the phone at the first ring and answered, "Hello, Ms. Precious. You were on my mind before you called."

Her phone conversation went like this:

> *O dear:*
>
> *I'm sorry if I woke you up. I know its past midnight. I still can't sleep. My mind keeps flashing back to all the love letters and erotic poems you wrote me. The sketch of you riding me from behind was so real and memorable that I feel your manhood in me, even now.*
>
> *Do you really mean everything you said in those lovely poems and letters? My heart beats through them.*
>
> *I'm going to read your cards all over again tonight. They are now scattered on my bed like rose petals. I want to feel you through them again, again, and again. I want to make love to you while reading them. I want to make love to you after reading them.*
>
> *Do you really long for me that much or was it one of your ways to get me in your cold and lonely bed just as one of your various conquests?*
>
> *How deep and true are your words? Do tell me my darling because I really want to know. I'm dying to know.*

*It's so cold tonight and I need you to keep me warm.
My electric blanket is not warm enough to replace
your perfect body temperature.*

*How much do you need me dear? Do you really need
me like the air you breathe? Do you really want
to see the stars dazzle in my eyes? Do you really
want to fill my fountain with your endless stream of
love? Do you want to fly with me to the heavens?
Do you really want to climb to the peak of Mount
Kilimanjaro with me and cum dawn together? Do
you really want to play with me in the meadow? Do
you really want to travel down my milky way?*

*Please, answer me. Answer me, my love with your
sultry big succulent chocolate black lips . . .*

*Oh honey . . . If you really meant every word you
said in those poems, then I'm all yours! You can have
me anytime and anywhere: at sunset, at sunrise, at
midnight, in the garden, at the park, in my bedroom,
in your bedroom, at my balcony, in my kitchen and
in my laundry room. Yes, in my laundry room most
especially. You will soon discover why . . .*

*Do me in my shower, at the beach, and even on a
cliff. My darling, I'm all yours now. Do me as your
heart desires. Lift and spread my legs and see the
wetness within. Spread wide my legs and see how
erect my clit is. Shit, do you feel it? I'm sure it can
cut concrete. Shit . . . shit. Pardon my language . . .
Don't you want me O? I want you then. O, don't you
want to do me . . . ?*

*My goodness, the thought of you is making me wet.
Let me slip off this lingerie. I want to feel you lying*

close to me . . . skin to skin . . . Oh, I can see the desire in your eyes. Do you like what you see, huh?

All you see of me can all be yours if you promise to behave. Yes dear, if you behave like a soft and passionate lover, I'll give you all. I'll give you all of me. I'm like a cougar in heat and I want it all hot, steaming, and aggressive. O, I can't wait any longer, please do me. Do me now!

Can you handle it? Can you handle me as I like it? Well, if you can, then don't just stand there and stare at me. Come over and work me all over. Come over and do me. My legs are eagle spread, giving you a better view of my forbidden cherry.

Be on your knees and inspect it, Dr. Observer. Oh, I can see you smacking your big lips. You want to taste me right? My clit is already throbbing and my pussy is over pouring with juices, at room temperature, for you. It's your juice now, I promise you. Yes, dip a finger in me and scoop it. Hmmm . . . , and you love that, huh? I can tell from the way you arouse me to the core. Just continue to do me. Yes, I like it like that.

Aha . . . That's it baby, taste me some more . . . Dip your other fingers into me and have a real taste of my honeycomb. You will never find any better than this. I'm made just for a lover like you.

Yes baby, do me faster. Come on, don't stop. Dip your finger inside me again. Yes, just like that. There is a reservoir somewhere down there. Don't you want more? Go faster baby, deep, deep, and deeper.

Stroke me now baby; stroke my clit till your fingers are soaked with my pussy juice.

Gentle. Please, be gentle. Place your wet fingers in my mouth. I want to taste me just a little . . . Let's taste me together . . .

Yes baby, that's it, hmmm . . . I love the feeling baby . . . hmmm . . . Wait, wait . . . don't make me come yet. Just tease me a little bit more. Go ahead; lead me slowly to the tip of the iceberg.

Oh no! You're such a bad man . . . My real bad man . . . You got your two fingers stuck in there without telling me. Do you like the way I vibrate my pussy against your fingers? Tell me. Oh, sweet Moses, see what you're doing to me. My clit is all sore, swollen, and my juice keeps spurting all over your hand. Let me lick it . . . Please!

Oh yes . . . Oh yes . . . Oh yes . . . That's it baby. Now lick me, savor the taste of my juice. Shit, see how sweet it is. I know . . . Just keep licking it. Use your tongue to capture my clit, bite it a little, lap it, and make loud slurps on it. Oh no . . . You didn't just do that. Oh, I got a mean and hungry horny lover. How could you tongue and finger fuck me at the same time so perfectly? Now, you're stroking my G-spot. Slow down; slow it down a little and gently, O, just like that . . . Yes, yes, yes . . .

Baby, you're out of this world. You're doing things I never imagined.

Oh no . . . . Just hold on a minute. Please, just wait a moment . . . wait . . . wait . . . shit, wait a minute, damn it . . . Fuck, just hold on a minute . . .

I can't breathe. I need my inhaler. O, please wait. Just wait a minute . . . gracious Lord, I can't breathe . . . shit, don't stop. Please, don't stop.

Oh gosh!!! I'm at the brink of climax . . . Come on baby, fuck me, lick me . . . Finger me . . . Yes . . . Yes, just like that . . . Yes, my goodness, yes, yes . . . O . . . O . . . O . . . O . . . . O . . . Oooooko.

After a brief break, she recovered and resumed the best sexual encounter of her life:

I don't want to be a selfish lover. I know you want to satisfy me, but I want to feel you too. Lay back and let me take good care of you. Oh, your dick is so hard and throbbing. I can see the wrinkles all over your phallus. It seems like you're getting ready to explode. Don't worry; I got you tonight.

Hmmm . . . , I'm licking your precum. Quite a river you got. Let me taste you. Should I baby?

Oh, you're so filled with lust and desire that you can't even speak. Ha, ha, ha, ha darling . . . you're just speechless . . . that is how I want you to be tonight . . .

Let me get back to work . . . I'm working my tongue all around your balls. I'm licking, sucking, kissing, slurping, ooooh . . . You're getting harder every second. I'm tugging at your balls now. Nibbling it gently, rolling it with my tongue. I can hear you shiver; yeah baby . . . . I'm going to make you feel like my "Jewel of the Nile." Just hang on. No O, don't come yet. You can't come yet . . .

I'm giving you a BJ. Damn it my love . . . you taste so good. Moan for me baby . . . Tell me how good I'm making you feel . . . . you like it huh . . . ? You're going to love me even better than usual later.

I have a bowl of ice here. You will love the thrill by the time I use it on you. Just give me a minute . . . What did you say? You brought some whip cream too? Aren't you such a naughty boy?

Let's do 69 then. I'm lying on top of you now with my legs spread open on your face. I am giving you a beautiful view of my pussy. Your penis is at attention to my face, and ready for my devouring. Here come my juices my darling. I'm rubbing the tip of your dick with an ice cube while you're inserting a cube of ice in my hole. Oh . . . how I love the thrill. Do I thrill you, my love? Go slow babe. Gently please, my love. Yes, just like that . . . to the left . . . a little to the right . . . That's it. Just like that. Yes, you got it . . .

Shit, how long is your dick? I'm sure you're desperately aching to be inside of me. Just hang on a minute. I'm enjoying what you're doing to my body. You're so perfectly meant for me. You know how to turn me on, and make me go wild.

Oh, my baby . . . how I love you so. Yes baby . . . I love it when you use your finger to stroke my clit just like that with ice cube. Wait; turn around, let me stick you in me. Gently, you're too big. Ok, like that. My goodness, you're deep in me. Please, hold me close. Hold me tight. Kiss me . . . O, make love to me . . .

Oh no . . . I think you're cumming. Yes baby . . . yes baby . . . Oooh . . . Oooh . . . aah . . . O . . . there . . . that's it . . . yes . . . yes . . . yes.

Oh my . . . Did all that come out of you? You must have a factory of cum inside you . . .

What are you doing? Oh you're so greedy.

You want to eat me huh? Wait; let me open up my legs for you. Is that how you want it? You wouldn't let me come out of the reverie of that orgasmic explosion before you fuck me? No problem my darling . . . anything for you. Wait. Let's make the licking another day.

For now I want your dick to fuck me silly . . .

Oh . . . You're big. I need to lift my leg up so you can fit even better. Oh . . . yes! Now that's better. I am yours baby . . . Fuck your baby . . . Show me what you got. Yes baby . . . thrust deeper . . . Ok, like that.

You love this pussy? You want this sperm pussy? Then fuck it . . . Be mean to it . . . Don't hold back baby . . . . yes . . . yes . . . . yes . . . like that . . . like that . . . just like that.

You want to fuck me doggy style? Ok baby, let's do it . . . Yes dear . . . oh baby . . . oh yeah, you hit the spot . . . . Hit it real hard . . .

Aaah . . . . aaah . . . aaah . . . baby . . . oooooooooh . . .
my baby . . . . shit . . . . I'm coming again . . . you
coming too? Yes . . . . that's my baby . . . Give it
to me . . . . give me all my love . . . mmmmm . . . .
mmmmm . . . .

Thank you my love. I love you too.

Her bed sheet was wet. She was sweating profusely as Oko said, "My love, let's do it all over again soon."

She hung up the phone and bade him Goodnight!

Then, she heard Jeremy, her fiancé, pounding at her daughter's door . . .

She opened her eyes to the heavy rain-pour outside her windows . . .

Good heavens, it was all a dream. She was relieved.

She wasn't even in her daughter's room but in her own bed. Jeremy wasn't at home either. He was still at the recovery center, fifteen miles away.

CHAPTER 14

In every respect, Oko was her man. He was the man: gentle and extremely sexy. Although he might not have been in the same league of men she had dated up till now, he was different and special. He was more masculine, stronger, taller, and sexier with mesmerizing eyes that any woman or some men for that matter, would die for. She adored him desperately from afar.

Precious believed Oko's differences were his strengths. She adored his comfort and the ways he is secure in his own skin. Confidence has now met confidence, perfectly. She knew he wanted all of her. She knew she wanted more of him.

She stood up in bed and turned on her bedside lamp. She decided to write in her diary, a short note about Oko and her dream before her nerves betrayed her and forget the details. She was still soaking wet. She decided not to do anything about it. She was just nasty like that. To her critics or those passing judgments in truck loads, she didn't give a damn either.

Diary: Page 105-???
Date : March 3, 2013
To : Mr. Oko Kediri

Subject: Wet dreams with O, the man from the motherland.

As I write this, I'm all wet from a dream of you. It has been like that lately. It's now official that I couldn't help but wonder how awful my days would be like without you in me . . . I mean how uneventful my days will be without knowing you are thinking about me . . . Right now, I imagine you packing up at your art studio for the night and walking to your kitchen to make your favorite dinner.

You may not know this but I enjoy making love to you every time I dream of you. Right at this moment, I want a long walk with you and then make love to you in the shower thereafter . . . Actually, I believe I'd love to make love to you anywhere before shower, if you prefer.

I am wearing the necklace and shirt you sent to me the other day. I wore the shirt since yesterday because I wanted to feel closer to you while I masturbate alone. I'm very wet at the moment wishing you are near. I spread my legs so you can feel how much I want you, how much I need you, how determined I want to feel you inside me . . . , all of you in me.

I want you to tease me everywhere slowly, suck my hard nipples, play with me, until you find my G-spot But that is not the release I'm wanting or in need of . . . I want you to make love to me as you expressed in your writings . . . and make me scream out your name before I explode into a thousand pieces as you continue to savor in my orgasm. I imagined you so hard and ready to induce your own release as you slowly ease yourself into my wet pussy and presto, you are home . . . sweet home at last . . .

You can claim my sweetness, own it, and work it with such intensity as if we are clinging onto one another in a passionate and rhythmic love making. The faster you go, the more intense we become. I want to caress you. I want to make love to you. I want to kiss you. Let's make love. Let me feel and savor your thrust. I want you to spill your seed in me—I can feel your manhood rise with each sensation. Your movements become more focused as you grab onto me and hold me down to position yourself so that every bit of your fabulous penis is penetrating my very core.

I can feel you almost there; your voice becomes ragged and your thrusts more forceful. I welcome you as you explode into me, calling out my name, while you kiss my hair and pulling on it at the same time. I am engrossed in you and want to remain under you. I have been to heaven and you came with me. Sleep well my love, she concluded.

To be continued . . .

She drifted to sleep while still holding her diary to her chest.

Shortly thereafter, her phone rang. It was Oko coincidentally telling her he couldn't sleep and just wanted to hear her soothing voice before going to bed.

Oko had been alone and sexless for months before he started communicating with Precious. He was more than ready. He hoped one day soon, she would take in all his manhood and the reservoir contend therein. He bade her good morning and promised to call her in the morrow.

On Friday morning, Oko called Precious to confirm their dinner date, and that he would be at the city's public parking as discussed.

Oko really had no time to be nervous. But he was. He had practiced the moment several times as if preparing for a debate of who will be the next king of his village. He knew the time had come. She knew the moment she was waiting for had finally arrived.

Precious packed her overnight travel bag by habit, the contents were conservative, because she knows she would not spend the night, on a first date, with a new man. She threw the bag in her backseat and drove to the public parking garage.

Oko was at the public parking facility by 4:30 pm waiting anxiously by his 1972 Ford Mustang classic for his dream date of the decade. He had just purchased the motor car from a fellow student with deportation notice from ICE.

Moving with the grace of a princess, Precious, walked toward him. As expected, she was beautiful and stunningly gorgeous. Her legs were smooth and long aided by her stilettos. Her physique was simply fabulous. Her dress fitted her curves. Her tank top showed her perfectly developed breasts. At the same time, she left a lot of imagination to be desired. Her attire was perfect for the time and occasion. After all, it was the end of spring. She wore everything well for the season like a runway model.

Her hair was flowing with curls and her softs, full lips, were covered with a slight rose lipstick to accentuate her skin tone. As she stood in front of him, she knew he had been eyeing her as she walked towards him as if salivating over the sweetest berry. In fact, he knew she was the sweetest berry that should be tasted sooner than later . . . She knew his desires. She was never short of self-confidence. Some of her friends despised her for it, but concluded, "That was their tough cookie."

Frankly speaking, the good Lord had been good to her; Oko was just privileged to have a front row ticket seat to view her beauty.

As Oko walked toward her, he gazed into her eyes as they stood still for a second or two to regulate their temperatures and admire one another. By all indications, they would have been

"Ready to rumble" at any moment if the location had been right, and it wasn't their first meeting . . .

They walked to the passenger side of his car and stood still again for what seemed like hours. They nervously hugged each other as if long lost family members just reunited.

Oko held her hand, gazed into her eyes and led her to the front seat. They admired one another again . . . Both looked refreshing and wanting. They realized their palms were sweating after a brief hand-holding . . . If Jesus Christ had paid them a visit at that moment, for the fulfillment of the second coming, they wouldn't give a damn. They had all they wanted—togetherness, face to face.

The way he held and touched her with his soon to be famous magical fingers, made her heart skip a beat. "Jesus, he had me," she told herself.

As they exited the parking garage, he cleared his throat and spoke at length about himself: he spoke about how he came to America on a visiting visa and currently working on his master's degree. How he would prefer to stay in America and be gainfully employed so that he could do great things for his village people and country of his birth. He also wanted to make a difference to the American society, specifically youth education. Oko had told her this story before. He was just trying to chit-chat and regain his composure because the lady he wanted so desperately, for so long, many nights, was sitting beside him, hot and smoky.

She spoke about her life too: her daughter, her divorce, her education, her fiancée, Jeremy, and all she wanted to achieve in life including finding a good Christian man to love and be loved by. She was just fishing for words to put Oko at ease too because the man she wanted was also sitting beside her . . . They both have identical dreams.

The sky was rich blue, making it a perfect drive for the August lovers.

The car ride to Oko's apartment seemed to take forever, she thought. Maybe, a jet ride would have been the perfect substitute for the occasion. They had one secret motive on their minds: steamy sex. Dinner was only a prelude to the end game.

Patience is now a rare commodity in both camps. As a matter of fact, she would rather go straight to love making than dinner. Food was farther away from her mind. Love protocol will have to prevail this time, however. It's the respectable things to do . . . after all, humans are pretentious beings.

They drove without music. They wanted to know each other. Although Oko wanted to hold her hand and kissed it, he was afraid she would reject his advances. On the other hand, She wondered why he hadn't attempted to kiss her on the lips or at least hold her hand.

Approaching Oko's apartment, it was raining heavily, her perfect weather. His apartment parking lot was flooded. His area was always flooded within ten minutes of rain drops. Thanks to low income housing project which the city can't afford to renovate or maintained due to budget cuts for the last seven administrations. The residents complained about their problems to deaf ears at the city hall and/or to their congress persons. By now, the residents ought to know their votes never counted. Oko and other tenants were part of the 15 percent of the 47 percent of the population the politicians talked about. On the other hand, the city has its own plan for the neighborhoods . . . potential investors from the east coast are coming soon . . . very soon.

They sat in the car waiting for the rain to subside. It felt almost forever. After five minutes of waiting, Oko turned to Precious and said, "Look my dear, I have a dinner date and no rain is going to delay that." He got out of the car and walked to the passenger side. He opened her door, asked her to cover her head with one of his art work, and carried her across the parking lot, and up three flights of stairs to his apartment. He didn't have an umbrella in his car. He always ran to his destination when it rained. He never thought he would need an umbrella for a gorgeous lady and a dinner date.

His nosy neighbor, Ivory, occupying the unit underneath his apartment thought they were nuts or drunk to their eye balls. They were drunk alright: with anticipated hot sex. Oko cared less about his busy body of a neighbor.

By coincidence, Oko finally had the chance to be close and personal with Precious. He inhaled her faded perfume, and for the first time, viewed her beauty as his cheek touched her soft skin. He was breathing heavily from just being close to all the assets she possessed—the assets he wished had belonged to him exclusively for months.

"You can put me down now," she said, as they got in front of his door. Oko ignored her directives and said, "Please, get the key out of my right pocket." He loved their togetherness . . .

For the first time, she met her match. Oko had become the man she had dreamt about. At least, for the moment, he was strong and possessive. She liked that. She liked that a lot in her men. She liked it even more in Mr. Oko.

He led her to the bathroom to dry off. Without anything fitting to wear, he offered her his oversized pajama pant and a blue T-shirt. Even in a simple ensemble, Precious looked beautifully stunning, especially when wet. Her wetness brought out her soft silky skin. She was like an innocent African virgin nurtured to perfection and fit for a prince, or ready to be delivered in a pre-arranged marriage to a village chief's son, working for the government in the capital city—fresh, clean, pure, and sexy.

In Oko's mind, she was the queen that must be his. He prayed silently for his wish to come true—to have her in earnest. Oko loved one aspect of Precious: she never wears a lot of jewelry. He likes her natural beauty. To him, there is no need for her to embellish God's perfect creation . . .

Precious always has a change of clothes in her travel bag in case of emergencies. This time, however, her personal effects were in her overnight bag, in her car, parked at a public parking garage seventy five miles away, in the city of OldPort. Again, she may not need them for the evening.

With the rain, Oko had been blessed with the holy water because the water from the heavens has made him and Precious closer and connected faster than expected. He kissed her gently on the cheeks, hugged her for a while, looked into her eyes, and said, "Prie, welcome to my home."

Oko was ready to prepare his favorite Ghanaian's Banku and peanut butter soup for his special guest. In his native land, they call the dish "Nkatsenkwan."

He invited her to join him in the kitchen and share the preparation of his delicacy. To him, cooking is romantic and sexual, and never an obligation. To him, he wanted to cook for her in the name of love, even though, in his native land, women do most of the cooking. He admitted that he has to get used to the idea of cooking, at least, his native cuisine for his lovely Precious. He's in America now.

Traditionally, in Ghana, the ability to properly prepare peanut butter-soup is the final proof of a woman's culinary achievement and readiness for marriage. If the soup isn't properly prepared, it could become a laxative when consumed. On the other hand, if a bride to-be could prepare the soup as it should be, for her would-be groom, it became a testament that she is ready for a lasting marriage. On the other hand, inability to prepare a proper peanut butter-soup was an automatic disqualification for marriage and an indication to the groom and his family that the bride isn't ready to take care of her husband during marriage.

In ancient times, tales had it that some young brides on the advice of their mothers had deliberately inadequately prepared peanut butter soup for their grooms just to escape pre-arranged marriages or a sure way to reject unwelcome courtship.

It is apparent that in many African countries, a man's litmus test to marry, among other rituals, is through his stomach. In Ghana, it was through an authentic and properly prepared peanut-butter soup.

Oko began to prepare the peanut-butter soup and Banku under the watchful eyes of Precious as they sipped red wine and listening to the music of Nigerian's best, Fella Anikulapo Kuti's *Lady,* playing in the background.

She asked Oko to tell her the soup's ingredients and the meaning of the song.

Peanut butter soup ingredients:

- *Beef and chicken (cut to size)*
- *Dried shrimp (powdered)*
- *Onions*
- *Red pepper*
- *Tomato paste or fresh tomatoes (purified)*

- *Palm oil or vegetable oil (palm oil recommended)*
- *Salt*
- *Peanut (ground and creamy) or peanut butter*
- *Curry powder*
- *Magi (bullion) cube—optional.*
- *Water*

Preparation:

Ingredients are mixed and boiled at a medium heat for about two hours.

Side dish: This is optional but highly recommended

Fresh Okra is chopped, cooked with a dash of salt to taste, at medium heat for three minutes.

The Banku (boiled corn dough) ingredients:

Corn or grain
Margarine or butter
Salt
Water

Preparation:

The corn or grain, unfiltered, is mixed with water, and salt to a smooth paste. It's cooked on the stove and stirred continuously to avoid lumps until desired dough-like texture is achieved. It's then molded into balls to be served hot or cold. A dough mixer can be used instead.

How served:

> *Banku is served on a plate with the peanut-butter soup with or without the okra.*

Banku dough is cut with three fingers, into appropriate size that can be swallowed at one time. It's then dipped into the peanut-butter soup with or without the okra, and swallowed (not chewed).

Eating Banku is an acquired taste.

Before the advent of china plates, Banku and peanut-butter soup were served in local calabashes. Many swear to their gods that Banku and peanut butter soup in a calabash tasted better.

For lower middle class to upper class or those who consider themselves to be well-to-do Ghanaians at any class, Banku and peanut-butter soup are now served on separate china plates respectively—in Africa, the continent purported to be die-hard on culture, foreign products are now the preferred choices.

In Ghanaian way, Oko showed his pretty Precious, how to eat the Banku with his fingers. Consciously, and in her normal sexual manner, she licked the soup off Oko's fingers. He showed her how to use her fingers to cut the Banku. In turn, she practiced her new acquired craft for her man, and fed him.

To her, to love a man is to love his culture. She learned that from her mother and in her humanity classes. Yes, she got the highest grades in those classes.

The dinner was for the lovers' book. It was simply the best. They shared a bottle of "Oguro," (local natural palm wine from the earth) as they sat on the couch in his dimmed blue-light living room. Player . . .

After dinner, Oko played another classic song by Fela Anikulapo Kuti, *Open and close.* He showed her how to dance the "Fire dance." They danced together and probably lost five pounds in the process. For both, it was "The best of times." They were laughing, joyous, and simply happy. Falling in love was truly great. He tried to explain the meaning of the song to her . . .

Within minutes, both fell asleep on the couch. The heavy Banku with glasses of Oguro wine will do that to anyone.

Two hours later, he woke up Precious and said, "It's getting dark Prie. I need to get you back home. I'd love to keep you with me, but a promise is a promise." He knew he was lying. What a player. He had prayed to God for Precious to stay.

She hesitated for a second, stood up, and asked for her clothes so that she could get ready for the seventy five miles ride back to her lonely home. She really wished she didn't have to leave.

Her daughter, Alice was away in college. Jeremy, her fiancé, was at rehab. School classes were over. She had all the free time in the world. "Shit, I forgot, I still have to go to work on Monday morning," she told herself.

She had wished Oko had asked her to spend the night. For the first time in her life, she would have followed his command. She just wished he had asked. Oko probably read her mind. He wanted to be a gentleman, for now. To sacrifice for love, he agreed to take her back.

Reluctantly, he drove her back to the parking garage in OldPort. Upon arrival, he let her out of the car, touched her cheeks, and kissed her gently. This time, he kissed her with all the passion he had bottled up for months.

He whispered into her ears, "Thanks for the dinner. Your company made the food tastier. Your company makes me the happiest man on earth. I hope we can do it again soon and more often."

She responded by holding his head with her palms, kissed him as if she wanted to make love to him on the hood of his car. Her heavy breathing was becoming uncontrollable. She was moist, wet, and ready to be fucked any which way legally possible. Even if illegal, she was willing to suffer the consequences. She knew there might be security cameras in the parking facility and thus changed her nasty thoughts. "Shit, we are all living in the new world, after 911 . . . ," she concluded.

Oko knew she was ready while they kissed. The day he had waited for had arrived and almost over. He had always done well in his probability theory tests. As such, the probability of fucking her that evening was 99.99 percent and the possibility of making her his own for life was 51 percent. Not bad statistics by any measure.

Then, he thought to himself:

> *I want her but not in this parking lot. I want to make love to her like a virgin: gentle, tender, slow, passionate, and with care. I want to kiss her from her head to her belly button. I want to gently stroke her pussy walls so that I can enter her with pleasure. I want her to enjoy the pleasure we both wanted and deserved.*

Precious started to shiver out of control but continued kissing him as if she was going all out for the Oscars in the kissing category . . .

Out of nowhere, Oko said, "Dear, I'm taking you back with me to Richmond."

"Thank heavens, I thought you would never ask," She responded.

This time around, he drove her car. She knew the road. She knew the hideouts of the highway patrol. She made the journey in fifty one minutes flat. It would take a law abiding driver, one hour and forty-five minutes. Sex anticipation probably contributed to some excessive speed and accidents on our highways today . . . her conclusion is not scientific by any means but convincing nonetheless . . .

Upon arrival in his apartment, Oko offered her a glass of wine and started the shower in earnest to get to the right temperature. Within minutes, he turned around, went back to the living room, and said, "My sweet, let me take off your clothes. I want to adore you naked like a water goddess." Precious did not utter a word. She was already in her pushed up bra and thong before he came back from the bathroom. She was prepared. She was known to be aggressive in the love department. She was breathing heavily and ready to fuck him with passion on his living room's white couch by the door. She does wonders with a couch.

He slowly kissed her neck, her cleavage, as he unclipped her bra to release her 36D breasts with hard nipples, waiting to be sucked. His lips found her nipples and sucked them interchangeably. He grabbed both bountiful bosoms together and sucked them. "Double pleasure, ladies," he said to himself . . . Awesome!

For the first time, she spoke, "I like that. Ummm, I like that very much."

Precious tried to control her nasty self, and failed. Frankly, nothing else really mattered. She loved the way he made her feel. Her ship had finally arrived with Captain Oko at the control.

"O, take me as you wish," she told him with incoherent speech. With her signature traits, she mesmerized Oko with her bedroom eyes so much so that he almost asked her to marry him.

They never made it to the shower. The water kept running and unconsciously providing musical sounds of its own. To him, the water bill was not a factor—it came free with his monthly apartment lease.

Precious pushed him into the white couch and palmed his bulging penis in his tight jeans. She unzipped the jeans and stroked his dick as if she was uprooting a delicate endangered flower for the Queen's courtyard. She wrapped her legs around his waist, and directed his dick into her pussy. Like a seesaw they made love like an angry Lions devouring their prey. For more than ten minutes, she held him as tight as she could before she exploded. He held her equally tight as he delayed his own ejaculation.

Oko was considerate. He wanted to please her just as he envisioned it. He wanted to savor the moment a little longer. To reduce his urge to ejaculate, he pulled his dick out and rested it outside her pussy as she continued to shake from orgasm that seemed to last forever. She kissed him with passion to be remembered. She had long waited for the moment . . .

The white couch was drenched and stained from her juicy juice. He just smiled and said, "Hope you wouldn't mind seeing that spot forever? It would be our reminder of our first time." She smiled and simply said, "You're nasty but I need to clean that." "Love, leave that alone. I want to look at it each morning," he said.

Oko held her hand and they went to the bedroom. She took control this time again. She was always like that. It was a bad habit that all her men loved. Her love making made them come alive from within. It's not surprising that all the men in her life continued to want a piece of her, under all circumstances.

Precious kissed every part of his body. She nestled her way toward his loins. She stroked and kissed him again and again. She licked him everywhere possible and massaged the entire length of his erection, muscle by muscle.

What he never said in words, his body told her in love making rhythms. His grunts and sounds were becoming louder. He pulled her up and kissed her fingers one at a time and moved his fingers to her red triangle to play with her clit and watched her "Melt in his hands and not in his mouth." The melting in his mouth will come in due course. Eleven minutes later, she did exactly that—her pussy melted in his mouth.

She wanted his dick in her. "Do me babe," she shouted.

"Not yet, pretty Prie. I want to savor this moment. You've a good Obo," he replied.

"What did you just call me?" She asked.

Sorry dear, "Obo means vagina in my mother's tongue."

His promise to wait didn't last long. His erection had been pointing at 180 degrees for the last six hours. His promise, "I'll wait," couldn't wait any longer.

Oko made love to her as if playing an expensive violin on loan from the Kennedy Center—gently and handled with care. He fine-tuned her moans and cries of ecstasy into his own orchestra.

To him, true love making should be slow, soft, passionate, and gentle like Barry White's *Love serenade*.

"Excuse me for a second Prie," he said as he got up and went to the kitchen. He poured two fingers of Passport Scotch—a blend of Scotch whisky into a wine glass and carried it back to the bedroom. He dipped a caramel covered stick of red lollipop into the whisky and gently massaged her clit with it.

"O, it burns but don't stop," she said.

Within minutes, she was moaning and shaken from ecstasy. It was her first with such potent multi-orgasm within one hour. Before Oko could say "Prie . . . ," she lifted Oko's hand from her pussy and placed the wet and aromatically mixture of caramel, whisky, sugary lollipop syrup, and her juicy juice into her mouth and enjoyed the heavenly taste . . . Oko then finished the left over . . . greedy boy.

Within minutes, tears started to run down her cheeks. "Prie, are you ok," Oko asked.

"I'm ok, O. I 'm just happy enjoying you so much," she responded.

She whispered in his ears, "You are Mr. Perfect, my darling." She was quivering from his touch and compassion.

He picked her up again and laid her on the floor for maximum penetration. This time, everything was perfect. They exploded together. She had stopped counting her orgasms after the fourth one. His ejaculation seemed to have lasted forever.

She asked him to lie on his back and relax. She put his rod in her mouth. Her tongue swirled around his cock and with the assistance of her hand; she pumped his penis one more time while she stroked his scrotums. Within five minutes, his dick was hard and ready—his entire eight or nine and half inch rod.

His jet black rod was the right size. Mr. Perfect. He was perfect in every dimension. She moved back to his rod and gently sucked and teased all his erotic zones until he called out her name through his raspy accent, "Precious you arrrrrrrr . . ." He had lost control of all that was ordinary in him. His nasty true color came out. "Yes, Oko let it all out. I like it so," she said aloud.

She had been aggressive with all the men in her life, but this encounter was different. Her tires had met the road . . . It was a hard contact but smooth ride all the way . . . It was awesome!

She allowed herself to be taken by him. After catching his breath, he took her by her arm and together they stood naked at the side of the bed. He kissed her and she repaid him in kind.

They were gentle at first, but as their kisses grew longer and deeper, so did the intensity and urgency to devoid each other again. She wanted to feel him inside of her, one more time. He wanted to be deep inside her just the same. Initially, their movements were slow in other to cherish the moment. Minutes later, their love making became accelerated. Their love making was purely raw. The speed of his dick accelerates with each deep thrust, as she sucks his nipples.

In Oko's imagination, he couldn't believe with all her sex encounters, and the birth of her daughter, her pussy was moderately tight. Or maybe, Oko's dick was too long and too big for her vagina. Whatever the reason, they were perfect for each other. That was what counted. That was what mattered to him. That was all she wanted.

Precious was wet. The urgency to find her releases overwhelmed her. She was calling out his name this time, as the rush to reach her release came so quickly. She could not control herself even if she wanted to. She could feel herself shatter into a thousand pieces as the explosion of her orgasm was too much to bear. At that moment, if Oko had asked her hand for marriage, she would have said yes. Timing is everything, Oko just didn't get it . . . he had failed to consolidate his dreams at the right moment.

As he felt her reaching her peak, he plunged his dick harder and deeper into her. He grabbed her hair; pull her head towards him, while reaching the stars himself. Suddenly, he slowed down . . . he knew how to control those crucial orgasm minutes a little longer: thirty-eight minutes and counting since they started this mutually inclusive sex encounter.

His soccer playing days had taught him how to hold his urge to urinate during a ninety-minute soccer match. He used the same soccer's strategy, experiences, and resistant training to control his orgasm a lot longer with Precious. He smiled and said," Thank you, coach Zanziba."

His release was core altering. Her body spasm was in rhythmic reaction to his orgasm. They'd taken a memorable journey together to the stars, and back to earth. If he had not been born again, he would have concluded that heaven is in his 1,000 sq. ft. apartment and nowhere else.

Oko wanted to please her. He made sure she is. She made it known to him too. She told him so, as she rested on his chest trying to catch her breath. She was hot and sweating like a cold frosted water bottle placed on a warm saucer.

They made love as it was meant to be. They were satisfied. They were exhausted. They looked at each other, kissed, and smiled as if to be saying, "It was a perfect fuck, wish we could do it all the time, going forward."

Oko hadn't made love for months. As imagined, she was not disappointed. He delivered his best. For the record, she remarked, "O, you're simply the best. Please, don't leave me. Shit, I meant to say, I hate to be leaving soon." Heavens, Oko missed another opening . . .

Oko and Precious made love numerous times during the night as the song by Lionel Richie, *All night long*, played at the background. The analysis of their performance will be another discussion, in another time.

Considering all that transpired throughout the evening, she pinched herself to make sure she wasn't dreaming like her recent phone sex in a dream. Oko looked at her wondering eyes and asked, "Prie, a dollar for your thoughts." She answered, "Nothing O. I just want to be sure I wasn't dreaming." Oko replied with his charismatic smile, "My love, nothing between us today was a dream." They both smiled.

When it was almost over, Oko, remembering her neighbor beneath his apartment, hushed, and covered Precious' mouth to control her loud screaming in case the neighbor, Ivory Smith (a.k.a. BJ Freedip) was at home and listening. He should have thought about it three hours ago.

His moral concern for the neighbor was too late. He suddenly realized walls may have ears. Walls did have ears because Ivory has been listening. She heard every performance, on and off the bed. Oko's Mandingo acts above her apartment made her wished she was the beneficiary of Oko's services that lasted all night.

Oko and Precious fell asleep with her back towards him. Oko's dick was erected and poking her round butt. Gently, he penetrated her from behind, rested his dick's full length in her pussy, and fell asleep from exhaustion. By the time they woke up early in the morning, the stage was set for the early morning love making. His dick was turgid and ready to perform brilliantly—the Mandingo had been in the house, all night.

It was Shakespeare who wrote, "What's in a name?" To Oko, Shakespeare couldn't have been farther from the truth. To him, name is everything. Oko had performed according to his name.

In his native language, Oko means Penis. Precious had been walking around calling Oko (dick) and thinking about it in her mind. If only she had known . . . Maybe, it was better she had not known. Either way, Oko had lived up to his name.

The next late morning, after breakfast of toast, scrambled eggs, sweet jelly, and orange juice, Oko drove her back to OldPort in her car. They promised to see each other soon. Oko continued his sketches of her. He wrote letters, cards, and religiously sent them to her every day of the week.

To his surprise, Precious refused to return his calls for over a week. According to Oko's record, she had ignored him for eight days, eighteen hours, fifteen minutes, and fifty two seconds.

On the ninth day, he received a letter from her enumerating the reasons she couldn't or wouldn't see him anymore.

Among other reasons, her Pastor had advised her to consider allowing her fiancé, Jeremy to come back home. She considered it and decided to make her unfulfilled love with her fiancé,

Jeremy works. She was just not sure of Oko, even though she seemed to love and wanted him.

She wrote him a letter of apology, stating, "If it was meant to be, it will be between us. I don't expect you to wait for me, but I'll always remember you as my best."

In addition, with sadness, she sent him the following poem she had read from an unknown author:

Man of Ebony

You have left me in an awkward position
You have made me doubt cupid's competency
How can you shoot your arrow once at me?
I thought love only comes once in a lifetime

Now I'm caught in the middle
How do I tell the true feelings?
You have wowed me with your words no doubt
You captured my heart with your words of wisdom

I'm caught in the middle of love and lust
Your poems stir up a feeling I never knew existed

Maybe it's in the harmony you gave me and the sweet
melody of your lyrics or the underlying meaning of
each verse

These are words I will die for any day and wish to
see it become a reality alive

You make my toes curl
Butterflies dance in my belly
When you describe your love for me

I'm caught in the middle
You had given me so much kindness
You have placed the world at my feet
Through you I have dined with angels
But had not tasted the sweetest wine
But you have gotten me drunk with a monstrous
longing to dine and dance with the angels
To sail with the stars to the Milky Way
To behold that which is forbidden
To taste the ungodly apple

I'm caught in the middle
How do I set my body free?
From the torment of your desire
From burning in this unquenchable fire
To sojourn on a journey with your fantasy
To unleash my untamed me that has consistently
demand to give.

I'm caught in the middle
How do I explain to the night?
And its cover has given me the chance to peer at the
moon. I wish for the stars to carry me to the arms of
the one who has ensnared me to his love or his lust?

I'm caught in the middle
Oh cupid, Where are you?
Why must I be your prey?
Why play on my emotions?
Why toss me in the waves of love and lust?
Why. Why. Why. Oh, cupid?

She enclosed a CD with one of Atlantic Starr's best, *Secret Lovers*, to express the pains in her soul.

The only contradiction in the song and their love connections, however, was simple: there was no happy home to mess-up in their lives: Oko's wife, who was still living in Kumasi, Ghana, had been fucking his best friend, and Precious, his new love, was struggling to stay with her live-in fiancé of nearly thirteen years.

She cried all night. It was a long night for both. Oko even asked himself during the night, "Why should true love be so hard?" Unknowingly, he started to cry . . .

Like a man with dignity and grace, Oko, simply replied with a sketch of them together at the dining table eating Banku together with a note, "I'll wait, my love. I have no doubt we will be together. I'll wait. God is my witness." He didn't believe his own words; he just had to say them for consolation.

CHAPTER 15

Two weeks after Precious' visit, and on his way to school, Oko ran into his neighbor beneath his apartment, Ivory Freedip. She smiled, looked at him, and said, "Good morning, O. You look happy lately." He cordially returned her flirtatious greetings and walked away. Ever since his opposite neighbor, Isaac, spoke about her as an open minded friendly married neighbor, Oko had decided to stay away from her, under all circumstances.

Ivory Freedip Smith, in her late twenties, is a beautiful young mother, and a devoted Christian. Although married to a traveling auto-parts salesman, she was a stay at home mom, raising her two children almost by herself. She had particularly devoted her attention to Oko's apartment since the day she saw him carrying a woman in the rain, and later endured the rumbles from his apartment beginning around 8:33 pm. Yes, she noted the beginning of Oko and company's joyous moments—one can call it invasion of his privacy. She called it joyous disturbances.

When Ivory realized the sweet forbidden act taking place above her apartment, she was probably saying, "Go O. Today is your lucky day. The jungle man finally scored," while at the same time, pleasuring herself with her sex toys in rhythms with the sexual sounds coming from Oko's apartment, unit 35C.

In the past, Ivory had complained to the apartment complex manager about barking dogs, drug sales transaction in the hallways, and loud music by the neighbors. This time around, however, the sexual melody from Oko's apartment, was tolerable and music to her ears. Cable television couldn't have provided better programming. Thank heavens; her children were spending the night with her mother.

She had once introduced her husband to Oko in one of their apartment complex annual Christmas parties. She always admires everything she saw in him. So did all the single women and not so single ladies at the complex. During their chit-chat, Oko jokingly asked her husband, Mr. Smith, "Are you related to Mr. Smith goes to Washington"? Ivory replied, "Who?"

Days later, maybe due to loneliness or maybe Oko was just so fine and irresistible, Ivory decided to engage him for a chat. She walked upstairs, knocked at his door, and pleaded with him to look after her two children so that she could run to the grocery store. Isaac, Oko's opposite neighbor, opened and closed his door as if Ivory's action was inconsequential to him. In fact, he has no logical reason to do otherwise. Ivory quietly turned around and said, "Hi Isaac", and turned around again to knock at Oko's door.

All Ivory did was drove around the block several times. She did go into a nearby Korean family owned convenience store once, chit-chat with the owners and their two-college bound boys, and bought one pack of juicy fruit, two packs of Twinkie, and two packs of M&M, in case, her children asked for the goodies she brought for them. She also bought Oko a family size bag of mixed jumbo nuts. Her conscience was weighing heavily on her soul. Her slip slope into the abyss of probable infidelity with a man she wanted was becoming a reality by the minute. In her soul, she wanted Oko if only for one night. She damned whoever he has been fucking—especially the day she thought Oko got his wings back. She too wanted to be served . . . Upon returning from the store, she thanked Oko for his patience and his free baby-sitting gig.

Since Oko's emergency baby-sitting, she diligently prepared sandwiches with side order of oyster, crabmeat, pecan pie, home-made chocolate cookies, and strawberry yogurt, for him as one caring good natured and married neighbor to a lonely bachelor from another land. She has a motive and definitely not innocent. Whenever Oko wasn't at home, she left the friendly goodies in a sealed box by his door with a note, "Hope you are hungry when you come home."

Oko recognized her motives but refused to take the bait. He wanted to be a devoted and righteous man with his honesty intact for his love that had temporarily gone into hibernation. He made one critical mistake; however, he always accepted the meals and acknowledged Ivory's flirtations. For a man of God, he was slowly selling his soul to the sexy devil beneath his apartment, one meal at a time.

One late evening, as Oko was walking to his apartment, Mrs. Ivory Freedip Smith beckoned him to come into her apartment for a second. She looked worried as if she was distraught and in need of listening ears.

Her sitting room door was wide open to project innocence. Her children were with her mother for the night, once again. She has been sending her children on purpose to her mother lately, since the beginning of the summer holiday, anticipating Oko will be at home more, after classes were over. Her perfect excuse to her mother for sending her children to her was, "Mom, I need to get up early in the morning to go for an interview." On this particular evening, her husband was also away on a five-day sales gathering in Baltimore, Maryland. She knew her husband's routine. She had ample evidence to challenge his so called conventions. She knows they were nothing but a rendezvous with his bitches but decided to suffer in silence because of her boys, two and three years old.

Her mother told her to be rational and ignore her husband's infidelity for the sake of her children. After all, Ivory has no solid proof and it wouldn't be easy to be a single mother with two boys even with child support payments based on her husband's current monthly take-home pay. What's more, she has no formal education or valuable skill beyond the one she performs in bedrooms. Even if she went back to work, she has no prospect of a good paying job. They barely paid their rent on time. She still relies on her mother for many of her daily necessary out-of-pocket expenses. Supports from her casual friends are mostly sexual. With her worldly possessions, she couldn't afford to pay for a sympathetic divorce lawyer with social agenda. To put it mildly, she was fucked all around.

"O, can I see you for a minute?" she shouted at him. She turned around and walked towards her kitchen, and added, "Can I offer you anything to drink," leaving Oko in the living room, still standing.

"How are the kids?" Oko asked.

"Thanks for asking. They are spending the night with their grandma today. Thank goodness, I do need the break," she replied. Liar . . . Her kids could win the best behaved children in the entire apartment complex. Even her two-year old was an angel by all measures—including the terrible two hypotheses.

Freedip offered Oko a can of cold American beer from Milwaukee and some cookies from one of those, almost stale, twelve in a pack, buy-one-get-one free, clearance sales, from a family owned convenience store, and said, "O, I know it's not my damn business, but I just want to warn you about the American women. Here you are—single, hardworking, in school, head on straight, nice, and so fine, if I may say so . . ." Freedip continued to pace around the room while still holding the cookie box to her side. She found herself nervous even after she had planned this moments many times in her head, in front of her full mirror. She was a little worried in case Oko's neighbor, Isaac, comes home early and witness what she might be up to.

She would still prefer to have Isaac as side order, when in need . . . She adored Isaac for his golden quality: he wasn't a greedy man and understood the extent to which she could offer her services. He had on few instances bought diapers and lunch money for her sons. Oh yes, he had paid for her manicure around few holidays. Sadly though, she also knows Isaac has his hands full lately . . .

Ivory stopped her little speech, gave Oko the box of cookies, and went back to the kitchen for her own drink of something liquid . . .

Upon returning to the living room, she was so close to Oko, he could smell her faded perfume. She was so close; he could see her nipples underneath her wife beater's tee shirt with the caption "Squeezable." She was so close; he could feel her heavy breathing and her swollen nostrils. She was so close; he had no wiggle room to turn around. She was so close; he could count her eye lashes. She was so close; he knew she wasn't wearing panties. She was so close her voluptuous chest was almost touching his lips . . .

Oko took a big gulp of his beer and nervously held on to the box of cookies as if his life depends on it. He started to perspire. At the same time, he was listening for Isaac's footsteps, in case he came home early.

She then continued her psychotherapy babbling session without a license, "O, please be careful of these American female vultures. Stay away from them before they drag you into their love nest . . . You are every woman's dream. They'll offer you cheap free sex to trap you. They'll seduce you to have your babies. They will do everything in the book to . . ."

Yes, if the truth be told, Ivory wanted to be to Oko all the women she warned him against, including the woman he fucked so happily, all night, weeks ago—she didn't know Precious' name. The only advantage Precious has over her, she believed, was her beauty. She equally believed she would outperform "Whatever her name," in the sex department. However, she forgot her reality—she had a bad timing because she had waited too long to catch her new side dish, Oko. She also forgot one minute detail about her current state of affair, she's married with children.

Ivory wasn't all that bad looking but she just can't hold candle to Precious' face. She knows that already. Oko had ignored her for months. The life sex act of two weeks ago, above her apartment, unit 34C, was enough evidence to remind her who is number one in Oko's life. Several times, she had prayed that Oko's nameless sex partner, of two weeks ago, would be run over by a bus somewhere in the jungle of El Salvador. What's more, Oko and Ivory have one common obstacle even before Precious came to the scene—Isaac. Oko stayed away from her because he didn't want to step into Isaac's territory, and Ivory stayed away from him because she didn't want to be considered a slot by Isaac.

Before Ivory could conclude her unsolicited neighborly warning, Oko was breathing heavily. He was in a cold sweat as if he had just completed a 5K run in an hundred degree weather. He was unable to stay focus, so much so that he dropped the box of cookies. He almost stumbled over Ivory's loveseat as he ran back to his apartment. He took a cold shower and later did what he had to do . . . Minutes later, he had a text message of, it was in your face, full figure of Ivory, butt naked: 36:30:38. Temptations, temptation . . .

Oko immediately thought about Precious and his undying love for her. Any future with her is now bleak since her goodbye letter. To this end, her love for him is a mirage to a great extent. Furthermore, he wanted to convince himself that any association with Ivory would be temporary; after all, she is married with children. "Don't think it," the rational side of his brain warned him.

"Ivory is a married beautiful woman with children," he repeated aloud about his aggressive neighbor, in the famous unit 34C. "What if her husband found out? What if her children found out and tell their father just as my own children told me about their mother's infidelity? What if neighbors talk? What if Ivory became obsessed with me, destroyed her own family, and derailed my chances of ever getting back with Precious when the opportunity knocks? Sweet Jesus, what would my friendly neighbor, Isaac say?"

These are some of the questions running through his mind. So far, Ivory has led him to the mountain of lust and desire. He had seen her nastiness and wanted some of it. To accept her offer or not is now the question his heart is negotiating with his uncompromising throbbing dick between his legs. "Lord, deliver me from temptations," he prayed.

It was rumored; however, that Oko's door was opened and closed after midnight. The nosy neighbor, Isaac Samuel Dickland, opposite his apartment, for all practical purposes, a peeping Tom; saw the one-way traffic outside Oko's door. He thought he saw someone of Ivory's height coming out of Oko's apartment sometimes early in the morning. He wouldn't swear to it under oath. He then concluded, "What the African mother-fucker lover boy does in his apartment, with his life, isn't any of my damn business." In a way, he was jealous of Oko . . . In a way, he hated Ivory for reasons he can't disclose to anyone, especially now that he has met a new girlfriend, Syndy, on the internet. Syndy, a divorced government contract specialist, lives fifty miles off the New Jersey turn pike with her, on again, off again, boyfriend. She could only visit Isaac the last day of the month—payday. She has one cat.

Isaac summarized in his mind, "What happened in Richmond, in apartment complex 1345 West Avenue, in unit 35C, belonging to its occupant, Oko, would stay in unit 35C. Maybe, if Oko is running for a public office, it would be a different matter altogether."

Since that day forward, Oko made sure he came home only when Ivory's husband was at home and/or her children were present. He regretted doing whatever he denied he thought he did. Ivory continues to leave him sandwiches and homemade cookies, once a week since she concluded there is no sign of his so-called woman coming around. She once asked Oko, "How is your lady friend?" Oko's only answer was "Fine," and sprinted away. Correction: he bolted away. Thereafter, he vowed to move to another apartment, far away, when he returned from visiting his home land in late August. He had sinned enough.

She continues to text Oko every morning, with the pictures of her goodies, especially her booty poses she knew Oko loves so much. Knowing what Oko has to offer, she wanted more of him. So far, so good, the arrangements were working, considering the fact that Precious had gone AWOL.

CHAPTER 16

Oko learned in a letter from his brother, Timbey, that his wife, Beatrice, had won a United States' visa lottery which automatically qualified her and her children a permanent resident status in the United States.

"If things worked out as planned, I'll be coming to America with the children in two months," his wife, Biola, had written him through his Facebook page since he no longer replied to her e-mails or phone calls. In fact, he no longer accepted any calls from that part of the world.

He wasn't expecting his wife to come to the United Sates. In fact, he didn't expect to see her anytime soon. He only wanted to send for his children . . .

The truth about his marriage must now be told.

Oko had gone home to divorce his wife so that he could be with his new love, Precious, among other matters. He knew for certain that marrying Precious would be his ticket to stay in America for good. He also wanted a new beginning, the third time.

Although he loved his children, he wasn't ready or willing to stay married to their mother. He had been blessed to have met Precious, who by all measures was his dream lady. To him, she was the most beautiful woman in the world. To him, he had met his movie star he read about, dreamt about, and wanted to be with, for the rest of his life.

The woman he wanted with all the marrow in his bone was Precious, his American queen from South Carolina.

He wanted to call his luscious Precious and tell her the truth about the rest of his past but she had written to tell him she was no longer interested in any communications with him for the sake of her fiancé, Jeremy.

Nonetheless, he still felt her love for him and his loneliness for her. All he could say in silence was, "What would be, will be."

He called his estranged sister, Mrs. Florence Shackles to discuss his problems; she too wanted no part of it. They'd been estranged since their disagreement about his unwillingness to return to Ghana after his first degree to be with his wife and children. "Lord, where do I go from here?" he had asked God in his daily prayers.

Precious and Oko saw each other in passing on campus. Every encounter was torture for him. They spoke as strangers to accommodate each other as mature adults. No one would have suspected they once screwed their brains out. He had the stained couch to remind him every day.

One sunny afternoon, they practically crashed into each other on their way to class. She had no choice but to stop and exchange pleasantries. She extended her hand and they chatted about nothing. "You look great," he said to her. "Thanks, Mr. Oko. You look great yourself," she replied. She pretended not to give a damn. Liar! She missed him dearly.

Oko had gained weight from stress, frustration, and countless bowls of chunky chocolate ice cream, he now consumed every evening.

He drove home with uneasiness. Instead of being jolly for meeting Precious close and personal, he was sad for the troubles in his life—the love of Precious, and the stale love he wanted to leave behind in Kumasi, Ghana, might be coming soon. He thought he might not be happy for the rest of his life for one love lost: Precious. The memories of her soft breasts and the perfect love they made together contributed to his pains. He drove a couple of times around Precious' housing development before heading home. "Living another day may be overrated," he once told himself.

Oko had hardly sat down in his apartment when his doorbell rang. He opened the door, and standing in front of him was his cupcake, tasty Precious. "Sorry I intruded. I know you wouldn't allow me to stop by if I told you I wanted to see you today," she said.

Before he could say a word, she continued, "I have rented a car. Let us drive anywhere to celebrate this day. I have taken two weeks off and I hope you will allow me to show you a piece of America and beyond."

He couldn't refuse her request if he wanted to. He was nervous like a child whose hand was caught in a cookie jar. He had promised himself that he would run to her under any circumstances. Even with prayers, he never thought it would be this soon. He was a man of little faith.

With Precious standing in front of him, he was whole again. His midnight macho thoughts, "Fuck her. I don't need her shit," many times immediately evaporated.

He invited her in and offered her everything he didn't have including the kitchen sink in his apartment. He was nervous and joyous at the same time. He almost started to cry. Shit, true love has brought out happy sorrows in him. "Thank you, Lord," he said silently.

Oko called his library supervisor to tell him that he wouldn't be coming to work for two weeks for family matters. He was not thinking of losing his job in the process, as a work study student at the school library. He should have honestly told his supervisor, "For family affairs, love, and great pussy." "Sometimes, honesty is not the best policy," he told himself, to justify his deception.

What an irony, Oko wanted honesty in love but had already started lying to have it. He was one of God's children, after all.

Ivory saw Precious on her way upstairs to Oko's apartment. She rolled her eyes without a word, and slammed her door. Precious only said aside, "What's with her?"

On their way to the car, Ivory was waiting outside the apartment. She held her younger son to her bosom and looked directly at Oko as if she wanted to say something, but instead, stepped aside and hissed. Oko nervously said, "Hi, Mrs. Smith, hi, Josh," and walked Precious to the passenger door of her car. Precious then jokingly asked Oko as they drive off, "What's wrong with your neighbor? I hope that's not your son?" She may be joking but close to certain facts. Oko simply replied, "Prie, of course not," and left it at that.

They packed and headed north. They drove through Maryland, Washington DC, and New Jersey. New York, New York, they went. They visited Broadway. For the first time, Oko learned that Broadway is a street and not a theater. He had a lot to learn about America.

They visited the Statue of Liberty, the American Stock Exchange, the Apollo Theater, the 911 site, the United Nations, and the Empire State building. They took the bus tour of New York City. They stopped in Queens and chat with the locals. They saw the hustle and bustle of Harlem, where they ate the best soul food on earth.

He took her to a five star restaurant to prove that he is willing to shower her with his American dollar. It was his first and maybe his last of flaunting his wealth in New York City after he saw the tab. The cost of one hamburger, small fries, a side order of apple pie, and a medium glass of cola would pay the dowries for two virgins in his village.

"Welcome to God's own country O," Precious told him as if reading his thoughts.

After that experience, it was pizzeria, tacos, hot dog street vendors, and all you can eat Chinese joints. She could only smile and said to him, "I told you five star restaurants are expensive."

As they settled in their hotel, he turned to her for a kiss. She responded with a light kiss on his cheek. She once again warned him that it wouldn't be a good idea to go any further.

He continued to hold her close, kissed her neck, and sucked her ears. Precious responded by grinding her midsection against him. Within minutes, they crashed into the loveseat and continued the fondling and kissing. Ultimately, they came up for air.

"No sex, not anymore," she said. He agreed reluctantly.

As she rested on his lap, he turned on his Kindle and turned to page 34 of Onyinye V Obioha's collections of poems and read to her aloud:

This Midnight Hour

If I don't kiss you tonight baby, I can't sleep
A screaming monster inside of me so deafening
Your sweet pouted red lips it seeks devour
I will smooch them so hard
Making them all wet right with loud slurps

And those juicy apples on your chest
How I'll attack it with raw hunger
Bringing you ecstasy like never before
You'll scream till no more
Until you're sated from my pleasure
Which I promise to deliver with great enthusiasm
I want to see you crawl on all four
And eagle spread your talons
Allow me smear fresh wild honey straight from the
bee farms of greater Africa.

I'll suck your thick creamy juice without straw . . .
A thick wave of curly black maze paves way as my
big black feeding bottle invade your red lips, and
wind you to ecstasy until you can't whine no more.

All I have on the menu tonight is my unleashed
ruffian they call him 'Maestro Phallus' the 'Mafia
Don . . .'

Just bring your yellow ceramic plate my sweet
cupcake and let me serve you something so good.

You can't resist this midnight hour . . .

Oko began to play with her silky, soft, black hair with his long fingers and at the same time massages her scalp. He started to touch Precious' face gently with her soft palm. He erotically caressed her soft lips and shin for what seemed to last forever. He continued to rub her shoulders and massaging her round full brown breasts without touching her nipples. He was good. Shit, he was very good. She told him so.

All along, he was sharing with her his life as a child in an extended and polygamous household. Oko shared with her the discrimination and nepotism in his family and the ways the well-offs in his family only protected their children at the back of the have-nots. He recalled the natural father he never knew. He told her about the love his mother possessed within but incapable of sharing the same with him and his brothers. He told her how he used to wash his half-brother's car three times a day for one meal a day. With tears, he told her how his aunt gave him, his brother, and her housemaid, four-day old boiled plantains, left outside in the garbage bin, where flies and maggots had their daily bread, simply to teach us not to waste food, even though, "I don't have fucking clue how the plantain got into the maggot infested garbage bin," he reiterated. He recalled how his entire wardrobe until the age of fifteen, consisted of two pairs of school uniforms, a pair of sandals, two khaki shorts and six short-sleeves shirts, two of which were for Christmas outings. No underwear. No toys. No birthday celebrations.

Oko shared with her, his best of times and many sad times while growing up. He told her about his brothers and the love lost between them.

He controlled his watery eyes when he narrated the ways some of his family members treated him like a servant because his mother was poor, uneducated, and without the wisdom or ability to bring him and his brothers together as a loving family unit, to this day. His middle brother had passed away now. He prayed for his brother's soul to rest in perfect peace, on the right hand of the Lord because throughout his life, he was a victim of a dysfunctional and unloving family.

He recollected the few in the family that cared, especially his grandfather who shaped his life and built his character.

He expressed to her how true love had eluded him until he found her. Unbeknownst to him, his tear drops began to soak her chest. He apologized and bent down to lick his tears off her chest. Before he could complete his narratives, she gently put her arms around his neck, moved closer to him, held him tight, and said, "O, make love to me . . ."

Oko held her up and walked to the bedroom, panting as if they had just finished running for their dear lives in a dark alley after they had been robbed. At the middle of the room, he held her close and kissed her softly from her forehead and rested on her lips for a thousand kisses, so it seemed. He removed her clothes one piece at a time and continued to kiss every naked part of her body. Like the act of an expert, he slowly removed her bra and licked her nipples, while she was using one of her legs to completely remove her own panties at the speed of light.

She started to remove Oko's clothing. She bit his nipples gently and moved to his underwear and removed it with her teeth to expose his bulging round and perfect penis. She held his dick with her right hand, squeezed it romantically as she sucks his nipples. Both were breathing heavily. Both were perspiring. Her legs were becoming weak and trembling . . . Her eyeballs, for a moment, seemed to be rolled inside the socket. They were talking but incoherent. They collapsed into the bed and continued the kisses and fondling. They lay parallel to each other as if they wanted to be one flesh ready to be placed in a capsule for space exploration.

Gently, he touched her pussy walls and found it wet and wanting. She looked into his eyes and said, "Please, make love to me . . . please, my love." For the first time, she said the four-letter word.

Treating each other like Jewel of the Nile, they made love. It was better than the first time. It was gentle, loving, sincere, and personal.

Neither remembered when they fell asleep.

The next morning, Precious opened her eyes, and realized Oko was glaring at her lovingly. She smiled and said, "Good morning dear. I thought we agreed not to make love . . ." Oko simply smiled and kissed her on the forehead. He then said, "Good morning, my love. What are we going to have for breakfast . . . ?"

On the tenth day, they headed home. On their way, they stopped in Washington D.C and saw the White House, among other memorable places. They wanted to capture the official residence of the first African American President. Oko was proud to have the same African connection as the President of United States of America. She was equally proud to have witnessed the first African American President in her life time because deep down, she knew there would never be another Obama or his kind in another hundred years . . .

On their last night in D.C, they dined at the Casablanca restaurant, watched the belly dancers twisting to the delight of men and women wishing they could do the same. They later saw the "Lion King" at the theater on M Street. Oko's only comment was, "Hollywood, Lions don't talk like that in the jungle."

"O, it was all a play," she reminded him several times.

By the time they got back to Richmond, they were both exhausted. She made quick sandwiches for both. She could hardly freshen up and ate her sandwich before she crashed and fell asleep in the spare bedroom.

As agreed, there will be no more sex between them until she could decide what direction her life was leading her. She was willing to be in denials until further notice.

Oko reminded himself of his own words once again, "I'll wait." Obviously, they have different definitions for the word, waiting.

———————————————

Oko's sister, Mrs. Shackles had left Oko several messages for the past weeks looking for him because his wife and children had arrived from Kumasi, Ghana. He was too tired to check his phone messages. All he wanted to do upon arrival from the memorable vacation was make Precious comfortable and hope for just one more sex session with her, in case she changed her mind once again, before leaving.

Oko was sleeping in his room alone, day dreaming about his love sleeping in the next room, when his home phone rang beside his bed. He answered it and said, "Hello, Oko here." It was his sister Mrs. Shackles informing him that his wife and children were downstairs and anxious to see him. Before he could compose himself with the thought of Precious sleeping in the next room, his estranged sister was knocking at his door as if the entire apartment complex was on fire. Oko quickly went to Precious in the spare bedroom and pleaded with her to remain inside.

He opened his front door, stepped outside, and immediately closed it behind him. He pleaded with his sister to take his family back to OldPort because he had a lady guest inside.

Since the Lord worked in mysterious ways, his sister agreed to do just that without a word. His children were crying inside a Chevy caravan in the parking lot, anxious to see their daddy. "We want to see our daddy . . . the children were shouting."

Precious was listening nervously from her room like a hostage behind enemy lines, but unable to signal her new location to the almighty Navy SEALS.

Meanwhile, Oko's children continued to shout, "Dad, daddy, daddy, we missed you," as Mrs. Shackles drove them away.

Ivory, watched in dismay, the whole episodes. While standing outside her door, she said, "The shit caught up with the mother-fucker." Her circumstances wouldn't allow her to join the family love affairs, even if she wanted to. Her husband was at home, temporarily. All of a sudden, she regretted knowing and preaching to Oko about American women. At that juncture, she said, "I'm such a damn fool," wishing she could take back her priceless commodity she had given up, to-date, free of charge to Oko.

Precious heard all the commotions outside Oko's door and later saw the visiting entourage through the window. Right there, she wanted the earth to part like the red sea so that she could be buried alive instead of Pharaoh and his army. "Moses, where art thou," she lamented.

She couldn't believe she misread Oko so poorly. Once again, she had lost the battle for love. She had lost the war with men from all places: in America, she lost to Jeremy. In Brazil, it was Riodiaz, and now from Ghana, Oko joined the gang.

Oko went back into his apartment and invited Precious to the living room for the true confession about his life to-date.

Composed, with teary eyes, she softly asked him, "What is your relationship with Florence? Are those your children? Was the beautiful lady I saw through the window their mother? Are you married? Have you been living double lives under my nose here in Richmond?"

Without waiting for answers, she packed all she could find of her belongings and ran out of Oko's apartment. She never saw that day or moment coming. At an instant, she hated her life, and hated Oko, as much as she had loved him.

Ivory, the wall with ears, opened her door once again, as Precious was running down the stairs, and said aloud, "You got what you deserve home-wrecker whore. Go ahead and run, bitch." It's so ironic how the hot kettle, Ivory, is now calling the smoky pot, Precious, black. This time, her husband was standing next to her asking, "What the hell is going on? The poor fellow had no knowledge of everyone with vested interest in Oko's affairs.

Precious ignored her and ran to her car and drove off like a maniac.

CHAPTER 17

Precious was still on Main Street when she was pulled over by a traffic police officer for speeding and erratic driving.

The officer said to herself, "Jackpot." It was the beginning of the month when some citizens believed traffic officers must work towards their ticket arrest quotas. With budget cuts and deficits, practically all the states of the union, conspiracy theories abound.

Before Precious could say, "Fuck you O," the police car was tailing her with the siren blazing. The officer got out of the car with her hand on her pistol, in case . . . Neighborhood red lining might be a factor for the officer to be that defensive even in broad daylight on Main Street . . .

"License and registration, please," the officer politely asked. While Precious was searching for her driving documents, the officer asked, "Do you know how fast and erratic you were driving, young lady?"

She started crying, and incoherent in her answers.

The officer asked her to step out of her car for possible DUI test. The officer couldn't believe such a gorgeous lady was in such a mess and might be in trouble with the law.

"Madam, bring out your license and registration, please."

Precious couldn't find the requested information. She couldn't find her purse either.

"Officer, they are in my purse and I might have left it in someone's house."

"Madam, have you been drinking?" the officer again asked. "No officer," she replied as she was wiping away her tears, sniffing, and murmuring as if she was under the influence of a controlled substance mixed with her drink without her knowledge. She looked a mess. Her beauty was still intact, however.

The day wasn't all that bad for her. Oko was also going after her after he found her purse on the pussy juice stained couch, in his living room, where they once made love for the first time. The flashing police blue lights and nosy onlookers drew his attention to the parking lot where Precious was waiting nervously for the law enforcer.

The crowd was gathering by instinct, to witness what wasn't their damn business. Oko never knew Americans are just as nosy as people from his native land. "We are all God's children, acting the same, everywhere," he told himself. The only difference between the audience before him and his people back home is the color of their skin . . .

Oko turned around and approached Precious with her purse.

"Officer, please get him away from me. I never want to see him ever again," she said while sobbing profusely.

All Oko could say was, "Officer, I was bringing her purse she left in my house, I mean, in my apartment." He had been told never to lie to a police officer; else, his ass might be deported . . .

He then turned to Precious and said, "Prie, I'm sorry for everything. Please, hear me out."

The onlookers now numbered twenty or so, were standing at a distance, under the command of the officer, to stay clear of her catch of the day. The rubbernecking citizens were slowing down the traffic as if Beyoncé was sighted shopping on Main Street.

The police officer was probably saying, "It may not be a boring day, after all." She asked Precious to take the purse from Oko and find her driving documents. She further asked her, as if she gave a damn, "Had he abused you in anyway?"

"Not physically, officer," she responded.

As the officer walked to her police cruiser to ID Precious, Oko was on his knees practically begging his Precious for an audience, "Please Prie, let me explain."

By now, the ever growing crowd surrounding them had divided into two camps. One camp was for Precious and the other adamantly against.

Both groups were dispensing unsolicited advice and judgments in truck loads among themselves. Additional onlookers became unsolicited members of each camp; delving into the business affairs of strangers they probably would never encounter again . . . Of course, more of Precious and Oko's color, spoke aloud the most. In the front line was Ivory Freebush Smith, anxious to know what will become of Oko and his hidden agenda with the ladies. She was pleasantly surprised when she saw Oko's home-wrecker, sitting in her car, sobbing, practically under police arrest in broad daylight. She then said, "My goodness, this shit is going to be good, bitch."

The radical onlookers in the crowd, on Precious corner, were asking the officer to throw the good-looking-dark-specimen of a man under the bus.

"He is a no good son-of-a-bitch, lady. You're too pretty to let him destroy your life. Officer, arrest the bum and throw away the key," WAWA members (wives against wives abuse) in their mist shouted in unison. One citizen from the great State of Texas, wearing a ten gallon hat, a belt buckle, a state of Texas tattoo, and a tennis shoe, shouted on top of his voice, "Hang him."

Just as passionate, a lady who looked like she had been drinking plenty of malt liquor, with a cigarette dangling at the corner of her mouth, shouted on top of her lungs, "I'm sure, the mother-fucker was probably caught fucking her sister." Of course, this self-appointed, alcohol brain-infested spokesperson had been a victim of the same fact and circumstance in her second and third failed marriages. She was probably the only one in the multitude, qualified to speak about the Maury show look-like episode playing right in front of the crowd.

"Men are dogs," another pro Precious concluded.

Politicians should take a cue from the small gathering and observe at work, how strangers can organize an emergency ad-hoc meeting for a cause they knew nothing about. No political party could've done any better than this gathering since President Abram Lincoln's administration.

A lawyer among the Pharisees and probably one of the remnants of the inner circle of Pontius Pilate also handled pretty Precious, her business card in case she needs an attorney. She specializes in domestic violence and animal cruelty—Cock fighting was her legal passion.

The opposing group (pro Oko, even though, none knew him or couldn't understand his sexy heavy accent) was advocating for patience. By their analysis, they'd concluded that Oko couldn't be all that dangerous. Otherwise, why was he still on his knees begging for forgiveness? One of the black ladies in the group even shouted aloud, "Shit, take him back, lady, he is cute as a button." A heavy set lady with a foreign accent added, "I think the pretty boy learned his lesson."

The police officer must have been enjoying the scene because she was taking more time than usual to verify Precious' information. After she had seen enough entertainment for the day, she walked towards Precious and gave back her driver's license and registration card. The last traffic violation she had on her records was a speeding ticket she received in Mississippi three years ago while going to her class reunion with Jeremy, in her former red Mercedes Benz sport coupe.

Precious should have known better to be speeding: A beautiful and sexy African American woman (colored girl as she was described on her traffic ticket), in a red Mercedes convertible on route 347, south of Mississippi, was every highway trooper's dream. Ok, that was the rumor by the unofficial club members of sistas with traffic tickets for-driving-a convertible. They called themselves, SWTDC for short.

The officer dispersed the crowd and gave distraught Precious a warning. She just couldn't see herself giving such a beautiful lady a traffic ticket since no one was injured. She waited until Precious drove away before she asked Oko to get off his knees and go home.

Oko was no longer himself. He had lost all common sense to reason. He got up and walked away in the opposite direction where he had parked his car. He was at present a lost kitten.

His pro group clapped and rejoiced for his freedom. To them, it seemed he won't be hauled to jail.

The police officer then asked him, "Mr., are you abandoning your car?"

Even a few of the self-anointed admirers of Oko were now murmuring among themselves, "That guy is fucked. Beauty and pussy had made him mad. He won't get any pussy from his wife tonight. The bitch is done with his sorry ass."

Sweet Jesus, Oko had lost his compass. His love for Precious had made him truly disoriented. For that moment, at least, the thought that he may never lay eyes on her again, made him sick and hopeless . . . He has lost two chances, to-date.

On her way home, Precious was sick to her stomach. She had been like that lately. Perhaps the stress of the day might be the culprit. She parked at the side of the road and threw up the entire sandwich she ate at Oko's apartment.

Like a prodigal fiancé, Precious wanted to go to Jeremy, her fiancé, at his temporary place of abode and ask for his forgiveness and say, "Jay, please come home and let's make what we have work."

She knew Jeremy would accept her before asking for his forgiveness . . . She had accepted her whopped life as her destiny. For now, Oko had sealed her fate against any other man. Jeremy will do. To her, "A bird in hand is worth more than two in the bush."

All of a sudden, she was tired of searching for hope. Reverend Jesse Jackson's "Keep hope alive" was nothing but a bunch of crap, she finally told herself.

Instead of turning to her sub-division, she drove directly to Jeremy's studio apartment on Jefferson Avenue and brought him back to her home for the final time. She had reached the end of any dreams. Oko had made the decision easier for her.

Jeremy just became the happiest man on the planet. They spoke for a while about the promises he had made to her and how he would make things work. Jeremy was elated and grateful. He confessed that he had known from his recent dreams that only death will separate them. He was right. He was always a man of vision. He had had the same vision before he was called to serve the Lord as a pastor.

He apologized to her for whatever he might have done, over and over again.

"Jeremy, please stop apologizing, for heavens' sake. What was done was done," she told him. She hated that about Jeremy . . . always apologizing . . . always accommodating . . . always compromising . . . even when she couldn't comprehend some of the reasons.

That same night, Jeremy proposed marriage to her. She accepted. There was happiness and hope on the horizon, in the mind of Jeremy, at least. He gave her the engagement ring he had been carrying around for the past five months—his grandmother's priceless wedding band . . .

They made love. She felt and enjoyed him by circumstances and not by the love she has for him.

He felt her with love and not by accommodation. For the first time, Jeremy knew she may be sincere to be by his side. Honestly speaking, however, his future with her is still uncertain. The only difference unbeknownst to him was that she was thinking of Oko with love and disdain as he was making love to her.

Comparing Jeremy's sex acts with that of Oko's recent sex acts, she said aloud, "I hope you rot in hell," while Jeremy's dick was pumping her pussy from behind. He ignored her comments. She had been known in the past to speak in tongues during hot love sessions. At least, she hadn't named names this time around. Regardless, he was not in the position to challenge or question her. He had just become an obedient servant whose existence depends on his she-master, Precious. He had just become mommy's boy. She was his M and M (master and mother).

She started to cry as they made love. He thought it was tears from good and compassionate love making they hadn't had during their inconsistent sex.

On the contrary, her life was full of hurt and disappointments. Oko was the latest perpetrator. "God is my witness, I hope he rots in hell," she said silently.

After all, she thought, she had found a substitute to Jeremy, in a man from a far, far away land. She had always loved men with foreign accents. What she ended up with, this time around, was nothing but a "deceitful, son-of-a-bitch, who is nothing but a horny-coated-smooth-talker African mother-fucker."

She hoped Oko would go to hell unannounced. She meant every word.

Before she went to bed for the night, she wrote a letter in a poetic fashion to Oko about the end between them. She wanted to convince herself that she had closed this chapter in her life and will move on:

Farewell: No More Tears

Tonight I shred the memory of you
I'm tossing the hurt and pain into the sea
Obviously, you're long overdue even though I failed
to see it coming miles away.

Your touch I will erase
You no longer set me ablaze
I'm done with the lies
It's time for goodbyes

Don't bother to explain
I'm not going to complain
The signs are in your eyes and the evidence before
me
You are as cold as ice to me. You are as mean as
Jezebel.

All those long nights I stayed awake
Wishing on the stars for your sake
You were singing her a lullaby
Don't even try to deny

I'm sure she is on her way home
Don't worry I won't stay
You can go and be with her
Life is never fair. I accept that now with sadness
But do keep this in mind
That you will never find
The love you always wish for

Because you can never have all I alone could give
I'm free of you without tears.

She was in love with him. She told him so. She was also in pain. She was looking to put a closure to the love she wanted but must leave behind.

Two days later, she went to her Wednesday choir rehearsal and made an appointment to talk with Pastor Shackles about all that had transpired. For some reason, she found herself drawn to Pastor Shackles in matters between her and Oko. She never told the good Pastor the identity of the real love in her life. Not Jeremy, she thought the pastor envisioned.

Pastor Shackles was a man of wisdom. He knew more than what she thought he knew.

Pastor Shackles had had enough. During their meeting, the Pastor spoke at length about Oko. He spoke about his hard work, his family, and most especially the friction between him and his sister. He sympathized with her dilemma but advised her to pray and leave Oko alone and let fate take its course. As always the case in such matters, they prayed together and hugged thereafter.

"I'll always be here for you in your time of need," Pastor Shackles told her.

"Please, don't disclose any of this to Florence," she begged Pastor Shackles. He promised never to do such a thing. "I love you and I wouldn't do anything to hurt you," he concluded.

She felt ashamed even more when the thought that Oko, the man she had made love to for an entire night was the uncle of

Samoa, the lesbian lover and partner of her daughter, Alice. The man she wanted for all the right reasons, was unfaithful to her, his wife, and his children. The man she wanted to love was just an ordinary man. At this juncture, all men are ordinary. Oko was just the worst of them all. She was disappointed that the man she admired for his wisdom was a fake and a fraud.

She cried each time she thought about him. Her pain this time was deep and hateful.

She wondered aloud how she had failed in all her love endeavors. "What would her enemies say? What would her daughter, Alice say? What would Samoa, her daughter's partner say? What would Riodiaz say? What would Jeremy say? Above all, what in the name of mother Teresa would Mrs. Florence Shackles say?

She forgot to ask herself one important question, "Where do I go from here?"

She knew she was not a whore but how could she describe herself given her history to-date. Her beauty and intelligence had come to naught. At her age, she was still floating aimlessly in the cloud, looking for love in men, everywhere, and anywhere.

To her, life has nothing better in store for her anymore. Her faith had betrayed, misguided, and forsaken her. She was ashamed of her destiny. She was ashamed of everything she stood for. To her, she was not as smart as she thought she was. To her, nothing mattered except to accommodate Jeremy and suffer in silence in other to safe face.

"Jeremy will do," she continued to convince herself . . .

She knew she was depressed. She also knew everything was her fault. She didn't need a psychoanalyst, like the famous ones on TV talk shows, to tell her that. Her brand of love, her definition for survival, and her resolve to find love and happiness, had proved to be beyond her reach. It was her destiny. "Jeremy will do," was all she could think about to console her . . .

"Oko, I hope you die an untimely death. I hope your dick falls off. I hope you burn in hell with only your enemies present," she shouted at herself again and again. She was simply helpless and defeated. She was hurting. True love had eluded her all her life, especially from her final hope, Mr. Oko.

She really loved Oko. She was in pain of love denied and has to settle for less to cover her shortcomings. That evening, she refused to pray before going to bed for the first time in her thirty something years.

Many nights thereafter, she would go to her daughter's room, close the door, and cry herself to sleep. She wanted to be alone. She was alone even when Jeremy was fifty feet away. The thought of just settling with Jeremy, made her cry even more. "All is history and behind me now," she concluded. "Finally, I will accept defeat," she ultimately said before going to bed, with tears.

CHAPTER 18

After weeks of loneliness, pains, and hopelessness, Oko wrote his Precious a long letter, explaining his side of the events that happened in his apartment. As always, she refused to open it. That was her way of avoiding issues in her life. She has not changed. She never grew up enough to face reality. What a pity. She was always her worst enemy. Like many of her generation, she will never get it until it's probably too late. She had decided to close that chapter of her life, even though, the chapter had not been completely written.

Oko's letter was typed, double-spaced:

Prie, my love:

I haven't been myself since you left me. I have had little or no sleep. I deserve all that is coming to me from you. My love, please hear me out. For your information, I have sent a copy of this letter to Pastor Shackles because, for me, forever, I have no option but to do all I can to show you my sincere love.

I'm not perfect by any means, but I want to be different and special in your life. I know you loved me. I hope you still do. I didn't know I would meet you but we met and we are here now. When I met you, I fell in love with you. I thanked my fate and the Lord for that. Meeting you is my destiny. You are my destiny.

I'm so sorry for what you witness in my apartment. Yes, I knew my ex-wife, Biola Beatrice, would be coming to the States but never thought it would be this soon. Yes, she is now my ex-wife.

I was married to her six years after high school. She gave me our beautiful children before I decided to come to this great country, for greener pastures. That was four years, two day, and fifteen minutes ago. I never wanted to return home. I sincerely thought my sister would help me relocate my family here as promised but all that didn't materialize. I wanted a better life for my family. I wanted to stay in America and invite them to join me. But my sister wanted me to go back home regardless of my hopes and determination to stay.

During my struggles in Ghana, I updated my plans and expectations and discussed them with my ex-wife. She supported me and agreed to be by my side. She agreed to be loyal to me just as I would be loyal to her. I was not perfectly loyal to her, but I was loyal. Unlike Jesus Christ, our savior, I had succumbed to temptations once or twice. You are not one of those temptations.

But one year and five months apart from my wife, she broke our marriage vows and had an affair with my childhood friend, Gonji Dudu, who was also my eldest son's godfather. He is at present a high ranking politician with lucrative government contracts.

My children called him "Uncle Dudu"

I found out when and how their affairs started in the two-bedroom house I built with my own hands before I left for the United States. I was told by my eight-year old son when I called home that "Uncle Dudu had been staying with mommy in our house."

I asked him for how long? All he could say was, "It was a long, long, long time, daddy. And daddy, they closed the door at night and asked me to go to bed because mommy and uncle Dudu will be busy talking to my daddy. Daddy, Daddy, when I went to pee every night, mommy was calling uncle Dudu's name in her room . . . Dudu, Dudu, oh Dudu, oh yes Dudu . . . Then Daddy, mommy started praying to God for help and shouting, oh God, oh God, oh my God, oh God . . . I think uncle Dudu was hurting mommy, Daddy. I tried to help mommy but uncle Dudu wouldn't open the door. Daddy, I know mommy was hurting because she couldn't walk too well the next morning when she took us to school in Uncle Dudu's new big car. Daddy, uncle . . ."

The housemaid also confirmed the same story as told by my son. "The children and me have been staying with their maternal grandmother over the past weeks since comrade Dudu came to visit," the housemaid told me.

What's more, she confessed that my wife had accompanied my so-called friend to a two-week Disneyland vacation in the United States. "Sir, did you see her in the white man's land?" the housemaid further asked.

I immediately called my wife who continued to make me believe she was in our home until I asked her to let me talk to my eldest son. "He is playing outside with his friends and not at home," she answered. She forgot, however, that it was 11pm in Kumasi at the time.

She denied ever coming to the States. I later obtained a copy of her tickets to the United States from my cousin who worked at a traveling agency. My cousin thought my wife had traveled with my knowledge. He issued the joint flight tickets to my friend and my wife. He thought I had invited them.

I was humiliated. Here is a copy of the ticket for your record, Prie.

I then called my so-called friend to find out the true story. When he picked up the phone, I could hear my wife's voice in the background asking him where and how he wanted his cold Stout lager beer. Of course, he denied the voice I heard to be that of my own wife of nearly eleven years. I was crushed, to say the least.

Several weeks later, I was further informed that my wife had moved to the capital city where my friend had rented a flat so that she could be closer to him, and away from his other two wives living in the local government where he is also the chairman. Here also is the evidence of the flat he rented for her and their cozy pictures, for your review, my love.

My wife never admitted to any of her adultery or provided explanations against my allegations. She never even asked me for forgiveness. Based on her version, she had no reason to.

To cut the long story short, I went home when you saw me off at the airport, among other things, to update my records with my ministry and also file for divorce. That I have achieved. Here are the supporting documents, for your record.

I never knew she would be coming to the States until she won the US visa lottery which gave her the privilege to come to the States as a permanent resident. I had nothing to do with that.

I love my children and I'm doing my best to be with them and take care of them. I know I'll try all within my power to reach that goal. I've been advised several times to perform a DNA tests to ascertain if my children are biologically mine. I'll forever refuse to do such a thing because of my pride, embarrassment, and the love I've for the children I've known to be mine since birth. Even if none of my children are biologically mine, then, it is God's plan for me. I'll love them the same, forever.

Prie, I'm so sorry I didn't confide in you any of these things at the beginning. Looking back now, I did it all wrong. Please, accept my apology.

One other thing you must know, my love, is this: I never introduced myself as Florence's brother for the simple reason that I've been estranged from her for the past three years for some of the reasons mentioned above. I also knew about the frictions between you and your daughter, Alice, and my niece, Samoa. I thought if you knew I was

Florence's brother, you would never want to be with me. I wanted you to know me for me first. Looking back now, I was wrong in my assumptions and approaches.

My love, I love you. How I felt and all I said to you about my feelings were true and from my heart. I hope you will understand. Please, understand.

Please, give me a chance to provide and explain anything you want to know about me. Give me the opportunity to tell you face to face all about me as I should have done at the beginning. I believe you owe me that much.

One last thing, I had written you those erotic e-mails through the Pastor's computer when I lived with them. My sister had informed me about the e-mails believing they were written by her husband.

I had since apologized to both of them.

As for writing them to you, I have no apology. That was how I felt about you. That was how I will continue to feel.

Prie, don't turn your back on me. I've come to you in good faith even though I entered through the wrong door. I've come to you with all the love in me.

My only love, please forgives me as our Lord Jesus forgave us our sins on the cross . . .

I love you always.

Oko N. Kediri.

CHAPTER 19

A day before Valentine, Alice received a copy of a lawsuit challenging the custody, child support payments, and visitation agreement made with Dr. Diick, a man that raped her at a dinner date nearly nineteen months ago that produced their twin boys.

In the complaint, Dr. Diick considered the original agreement between him and Alice hastily drafted, preposterous; one sided, unreasonable, and unacceptable.

In a way, Alice agreed in principle with Dr. Diick's complaint because from the beginning, she always wanted her boys' father to be in their lives. In the beginning, Alice and Dr. Diick were good friends. She cherished their friendship. They were both homosexuals, and the issue of how and where to raise their children in a particular environment was not an issue. Dr. Diick had kept his promise and provided for his children. Lastly, she didn't want absentee father in her twin boys' life as her own father was absent in her life.

Thirty days later, they were in the family court to resolve the custody and other matters.

For the love of Alice and probably for his regrets of how their brief relationship began and ended, Dr. Diick, for the first time, wanted to apologize to Alice.

To this end, he asked the court for permission to address Alice before the court proceedings.

The judge considered his request and said, "Dr. Diick, your request is unusual, but I'll allow it."

He stood, faced Alice, and said:

> *Alice, I want to express my apology for all that has transpired between us. I never meant for what happened to happen. I took advantage of your trust and friendship and I am very sorry. I know you had been a great mother to our children. I will forever be grateful. I'm here to ask for your forgiveness regardless of what we agree here in court today. I love you and our children.*

He then turned to the judge and said, "Your honor, that's all I have to say."

Alice looked at him, nodded, smiled, and accepted his apology. She was only nineteen and eight months old. She was too matured for her age. Even the court acknowledged her maturity, efforts, and resolve.

The court then remarked, "You are a courageous young lady and deeply admired. You are special and I wish you the best life has to offer to you and your children."

This time, it was a better reunion than the day of depositions nineteen months ago on issues that brought them to court this time. Truly, time heals, if given a chance.

With love and understanding in the air, the court directed the lawyers and their clients to arbitrate their differences. After a two-hour recess, an agreement was announced for the court's approval.

In the agreement, both parents agreed to the following:

> *They will have joint custody of their twin boys.*

> *Dr. Diick will have custody of his boys every other summer months.*

> *Dr. Diick agreed to pay for the children's education in public schools up to college level; however, the children could attend private schools if Alice is willing to pay for the difference in tuition, accommodation, and maintenance. He was a byproduct of public schools and he saw no problems in the system. To him, private schools had been overrated considering the ever escalating costs.*

> *He will have the children every other weekend.*

> *He will claim one of the children, Al, on his tax returns.*

> *Both parents and the children will have family dinner together the last Sunday of the month.*

> *Both parents must conduct themselves properly in front of the children. They must maintain healthy relationships for the sake of the children.*

> *The monthly support was reduced to $585.56 per child.*

*He agreed to relocate to the same city where Alice
and the children lived so that he could satisfy the
visitation agreements.*

*They will exchange phone numbers to improve
communications.*

The court approved the agreements and wished them Godspeed.

That evening, Dr. Diick, Alice, and the children went to dinner.
He missed his children and Alice knew it.

Alice went home after dinner without her children. She felt
good and vindicated as a great mother, even at her age. The
children spent the night with their father.

As soon as she got home, her mother, Precious called to inform
her that she was a party to a couple of lawsuits. "Who are
these people again? I'm fucking tired of this roller coaster,"
she responded.

"Watch your mouth girl. Babe, please take it easy. Try and
come over. You can read the papers when you get here. I love
you," she said. That evening, she drove to her mother's house
to obtain a copy of the lawsuits.

The first lawsuit was between the estates of Jeremy Warren,
plaintiffs, against the beneficiaries, defendants. Genesis and
Revelations, PLLC was the lawyer for the plaintiff.

The lawsuit alleged that the beneficiaries fraudulently enriched
themselves from the purported confessions and illegal digital
will and testament of Jeremy Warren, an individual who had
been in a coma for over seven months before his alleged suicide.

It was also alleged that the deceased, was so heavily drugged and sedated, therefore impossible for him to commit suicide in his hospital bed. What's more, he died in the watchful eyes of the hospital staff and the chaplain. In addition, the security cameras in his room showed no activities of a suicide. It was further alleged that Jeremy's thoughts were distorted, not of a sound mind, and thus incapable of legally dictating his last will and testament.

As a result, the suit asked the court to annul the so-called will, recover the estate's fraudulently distributed assets among the beneficiaries with interest. The suit also asked for triple punitive damages.

> *Michael Warren (father), Sandra Hurt—Warren (mother), MaryAnn Tick-Bush (sister) and Alexandra B Freedom (daughter), for the estate of Jeremy Warren.*

> *Plaintiffs*

> *V*

> *Alice Riodiaz-Shackles, Al and Sam Diick, Dr. She Riodiaz Dansford (formerly Precious Riodiaz), Moji She Warren, Samoa Shackles, Pastor Thomas Shackles, and Mrs. Florence Shackles*

> *Defense*

The presiding estate judge upheld the digital will of Jeremy Warren and dismissed all charges against the beneficiaries. All concerned, accepted the judge's ruling and agreed not to appeal the case to higher courts. Appeals cost money and time. The family of the plaintiffs had very little of that. The beneficiaries had practically gone through their windfall.

The second lawsuit contended that the defendants, Father Jones and his diocese, were negligent because Father Jones witnessed and didn't prevent the suicide of Jeremy Warren (plaintiff), on his hospital bed during his so-called confessions to him:

Michael Warren (father of Jeremy Warren)

Plaintiff

V

Father Jones and his diocese

Defense

The case was settled out of court for an undisclosed amount. All dioceses have since revised their Chaplains' confessional standards.

The third lawsuit on behalf of the deceased, Jeremy Warren, was against the hospital and Jeremy's attending physicians as defendants for gross negligence, medical malpractice, wrongful death, and contributing to the death of a psychotic patient. The lawsuit also alleged that the hospital and the co-defendants failed to use due professional diligence and/or adhere to their professional Hippocratic Oath not to kill.

Michael Warren (father), Plaintiff

V

Main Street Hospital, Inc., the attending physicians: Dr. Burstein, Dr. Wong, and Dr. Olawole; the Nursing Directors and the entire nursing staff; the pharmacy, the maintenance department, and

> *the hospital's hospitality department including the*
> *cafeteria staff, defense*

The case went to arbitration and was settled out of court for an undisclosed infinitesimal amount.

The court proceeding was emotional and troubling for everyone involved, stemming from the fact that most of the loots received by the beneficiaries had been spent or gifted away.

Most shocking was the revelation, after DNA results, demanded by the plaintiffs from all defendants, that Moji Precious Warren, the daughter of Precious Riodiaz Dansford was not the biological daughter of Jeremy Warren, deceased.

"Whose child was she?" was the question everyone was asking. The rumor mill about Precious' indiscretions was once again in full force.

All the men in Precious' life, a year before Moji was born, were required to take a DNA test. They included Pastor Shackles, Riodiaz, Oko, and Elder Pokerville, the chair of the deacon board; whom she dated briefly before securing her position as the Music director. Many volunteered for the DNA test because they wanted to be with her and her daughter.

Oko's DNA was a perfect match as Moji's biological father.

Only two people knew the true parents of Moji—Dr. Precious Riodiaz Dansford and Pastor Shackles. Oko suspected but not one hundred percent certain.

Precious knew this fact but her pride and resolve wouldn't allow her to tell Oko Yembe or confess to anyone else for that matter. She has one reason for her actions: she was engaged to Jeremy Warren.

It was now clear for the whole world to know that Pastor Shackles was not having an affair with Precious. The support by him was his attempt to protect her and Oko from his wife, Florence and their daughter, Samoa. He wasn't pleased about the whole family love affairs.

All the evidence his wife, Florence, had been gathering against his husband's supposed adulterous relationship with Precious was useless and pointless. If she had known the facts, she should have listened to the song of Tammy Wynette, *Stand by Your Man,* instead of chasing a false rainbow as shown to her by her so-called friends and self-appointed secret intelligent agents.

It was also clear that the heated arguments on the telephone between Precious and the unknown caller, overheard by her ex-husband, Riodiaz, every night, while temporarily residing at her house was between her and Oko. Oko had wanted to know if he is the father of Moji. If he is, he wanted, at least, a joint custody and visitation rights now that her fiancé Jeremy was dead. He also wanted to rename Moji, "Ife", meaning, love.

Oko wanted Ife to fulfill his empty life and hopefully give him an opportunity to be closer to Precious at the same time. In fact, he wanted to be with her and his daughter as a family unit. He wanted desperately to ask Precious to marry him so that they could live happily ever after, as husband and wife, as the good Lord intended. He had urged her to read his letters so that she could make the right decision about him and their daughter. "We belong together," he pleaded with her each night.

Knowing that Riodiaz, her ex, was recuperating in her house was yet another issue discussed during their hot telephone conversations. Oko hated the idea that Riodiaz might once again be sleeping with his love, Precious.

He knew Riodiaz couldn't and wouldn't control himself while lodging at her house. The sight of Precious would make any man's dick hard at any age. Precious' temptation to succumb to Riodiaz's charm was another factor in his mind.

With a name like Riodiaz, he had wished he was an illegal alien so that he could call ICE on his ass and be deported within 48 hours or jailed indefinitely like those in Guantanamo Bay. He even wished on several occasions, Riodiaz has lived in the great state of Arizona. With a name like his, he would have been arrested anyway, on his way to renew his driver's license, and jailed for months before his lawyer could prove his identity and citizenship. "There wouldn't be a "Dream Act" for his fucking ass, citizen or not. Not in the great state of Arizona, where profiling reigns," was all he ever thought about . . .

At last, with the help and counseling of Pastor Shackles, Oko Yembe and Precious agreed to meet and iron out their differences for the sake of their daughter, Moji.

Precious called a few days later to cancel the meeting. She sent a letter to Oko through Pastor Shackles unequivocally stating, "If you want to see your daughter, meet me in court, liar." Precious will always be Precious, to the end. She wouldn't get. Never!

CHAPTER 20

In the final analysis, there was a mixed blessing in the new relationship between Alice and her children's gay father, Dr. Diick. The amicable end result was unintentional but better than expected.

There was a happy ending between Alice and Dr. Diick and their children. Their relationship became stronger every passing day. He made every effort to show his love to his children. He admired and respected Alice. He did all within his power to show the world he was the exemplary father he wanted to be. Alice was proud of him. He adored her. He admired her tenacity, grace, maturity, and was very proud of her as a young woman of only nineteen years old. He loved her as the mother of his children.

Alice and her partner, Samoa now had more time to enjoy each other when the children were with their father. They loved the peaceful time together. The sex between them was hotter, more frequent, and passionate. Samoa was a screamer. She was definitely a squirter. She was now liberated to shout during love making. Their little apartment had made it impossible to express their sexual pleasures with the kids around.

But there was also a void in their lives of a sort with the temporary absences of the children they'd raised together from birth.

To some, especially her African born women, the greatest regret Mrs. Florence Shackles had was that her only daughter, Samoa, a lesbian, couldn't bear her grandchildren. Samoa had broken the family link and created a gap in her family tree.

She made her discontentment known to Samoa every time the family met for dinner. Florence was convinced "Samoa's situation" was her punishment from the Lord because she had not told her husband to this day that Samoa wasn't his biological daughter. "What else could it be," she asked herself. All she could do was repent to her God and pray for forgiveness.

One evening, after dinner with their usual glass of red wine before bed, Alice and Samoa kissed and made love on the sofa. The sofa had been reupholstered once already since purchased four months prior. They always forgot to lay a sofa cover on it before sex. Alice was always impatient when she wanted sex. Like daughter like mother, Alice enjoyed steamy sex, everywhere and whenever the urge came upon her. According to Alice, the sofa was the best place, for the best positioning, especially during their afternoon delight with a modern jazz at the background. Samoa pours a lot during sex and a few more aftershocks . . . Heavens.

Later, as *Endless Love*, by Lionel Richie and Diana Ross was playing on surround sound at a distance; Samoa held Alice's hand and led her to the bedroom.

Waiting for Alice on her side of the bed was a red panty, a red bra, a box of chocolate, and massage oil. Alice got the message. Alice led Samoa to the shower, bathed her and rinsed her off. She rubbed her with a silky lotion made from coconut and black soap oil. Goodness, the second act began. It lasted for seventy three minutes. Yes, they always timed their sexual encounters. They promised themselves that the next sex encounter would always be longer and better than the previous ones. It was a challenge they kept, enjoyed, and look forward to.

While Samoa placed her head on Alice's chest after their sex marathon, she said:

> *Love, please, hear me out. It seems we have to share our children with their father now. He is great to his children. The more I think of it, the more I know things will not be the same between us and the kids. As discussed, my mother wanted me to have at least a child just for her and her pride. What bothered my mother was not necessarily my lesbianism, but the fact that I wouldn't be able to produce grandchildren for her.*
>
> *Left to my mother, she is ok with everything but her culture is the driving force behind her point of view against it. Those damn Africans . . . My love, when you're ready, can we talk about what we ought to do? I'll agree with whatever you suggest. I love you, dearly."*

Alice turned without a word and pretended to go to sleep. Samoa didn't say anything either. They know each other so well that they communicate in codes, most of the time. To their friends, they would be considered weird, to say the least. In their little kingdom, they were just perfect. The rest of the world can go to hell.

Two days later, Alice prepared a special dinner for Samoa. Dinner was simple and delicious: a supreme deluxe pizza (served on china), salad, chocolate mousse for desert, and a glass of wine for Samoa and a glass of lemonade for her. Alice never liked the taste of alcohol.

During dinner, Alice held Samoa's hand and said, "My love, I have an idea for your consideration. Why can't we each have artificial insemination?"

"Excuse me, Alice?" Samoa asked.

Samoa had considered the same solutions months before. She hugged Alice as she cried and confessed how she had been worried what Alice's response would be since she brought up the subject about her mother's demand.

One thing was certain, true love existed between them. They always knew what matters to them the most. They knew love can't be ascribed to them but only achieved by them. They respect each other. They accommodate each other. They support each other. They depend on each other. Everything between them was unselfish, considerate, and loving. They never dwell on the negative comments of others; rather, they cherish what they meant to each other. They work so hard to succeed in all their endeavors. "This is our world and we will make the best of it," was written on a plague hung in their bedroom besides a full length mirror.

The next Sunday, during dinner, Samoa informed her mother, Mrs. Shackles, about their decisions. Mrs. Shackles cried, prayed, and gave thanks to her God Almighty. Her prayers had been heard without a doubt. She promised on behalf of her husband that they will cover the costs of the procedures.

In earnest, they selected the sperm of an outstanding computer and internet entrepreneur. The donor was financially astute and was also a part-time drama teacher at a local college. Oops, drama teacher again? Alice knew too well about drama teacher. Dr. Diick was a drama teacher and . . . The only difference was that Samoa's association with a drama teacher was planned and consented to, this time around. What's more, it would be an affair with a frozen sperm, kept in a dish.

On March 6, it was official that Alice was pregnant with another set of twins. Samoa was pregnant with twins as well: a boy and a girl. Alice did not want to know the genders of her babies.

At last, their true love continued to sustain the test of time. They rejoiced as they recited Philippians 4:4:

> *Rejoice in the Lord always.*
> *I will say it again, rejoice!*

Late afternoon in April, Pastor and Mrs. Shackles made a courtesy visit to Precious at her home. Mrs. Shackles brought her a plate of her favorite Nigerian bean cakes, fried plantain with sardine, red pepper, and scrambled eggs. Yummy, yummy . . .

Precious was shocked and pleasantly surprised as she welcomed them into her home considering all that had happened between her and Oko. Pastor Shackles led a brief prayer on peace, fulfillment, love, and forgiveness. They never spoke about Oko during their visit.

They officially invited her to their post Easter Sunday church service dinner in their 10,000 sq. ft. opulent parsonage.

Mrs. Shackles then gave her a hug for the first time and said, "Please, come early for dinner. I need your assistance in getting things ready. Don't bring anything except your fine self and my daughter, Moji."

CHAPTER 21

It was rumored that Pastor Shackle may be joining another church. He had been at the helm of his church for so long that no one believed he would be jumping ship anytime soon. Under his leadership, the church membership had grown from 20 to 9,456 registered members, not counting the TV viewing audiences all over the globe. The African and South American viewing audiences are growing leaps and bounds, each Sunday. No one knows exactly the weekly receipts of the church, but with an average weekly tithe of ten dollars and five cents multiplied by 10,566 committed registered members worldwide, anyone with simple Texas instrument's calculator will come up with a reliable figure. Of course, they have expenditures as well. The newly renovated mega church is estimated to cost fifteen millions, fifty percent financed by three local banks.

On Easter Sunday service, assistant Pastor-Mrs. Shackles introduced her husband with fifteen minutes of accolades, including the love she has and will always have for her beloved and sweet husband.

For the first time, Mrs. Shackles told the congregation that her husband had just been promoted to a Bishop. The congregation sang and danced the fire dance, as many African churches, do in motherland Africa.

The congregation went nuts with the loudest applause when the new minted Bishop Shackles, DD—former Pastor Shackle, approached the pulpit. The ovation lasted for another twenty minutes, so it seemed.

One of the oldest founding members of the church went straight to the altar and immediately demanded congratulatory gifts for the pastor. "If not now, then when?" she told the congregation. Within minutes, enough gifts were collected on behalf of the Bishop, to pay for a fully loaded new 2013 SUV Cadillac Escalade. The trustee board always wanted the best for their new Bishop. His current car was already three years old—image is everything.

In his new robe, almost similar to the one won by Pope John Paul, IV, during Sunday Mass at the Vatican, Bishop Shackles stepped to the microphone and acknowledged his congregation's love and support. More applause erupted from the flock.

With all the emotions, applause, and jubilations, he thanked his flock for their generosity. He then turned to his wife and thanked her for being the pillar of his existence. "I love you as Jesus Christ loved the Church. You will always remain my African queen," he said with a smile.

He then invited his daughter, Samoa and her partner, Alice, to sit on his right hand. To his left, he invited his wife and Dr. Precious Dansford, to take their designated seat.

He went straight to his sermon after the congregation sang a few selected songs from the hymn book.

Bishop Shackles' 2012 Easter Sunday sermon was titled, "My Redemption Oh Lord, For I Have Sinned."

Happy Easter, my Brethren.

I'm here today to humble myself before you. I want to thank each and every one of you for your kindness, support, and devotion to me, my family; this house of worship, and to the Lord Jesus Christ, our savior, and redeemer.

Seated on my right are my loving daughter, Samoa and her partner, Alice. If there is a stranger among us today, let me get y'all up to speed. They are lesbians.

Let me repeat that again. They are young women, and in love with each other.

Bishop Shackles allowed his flock to adjust themselves in their seats. None of the church's regular members saw the day coming and couldn't believe their ears. Some visiting guests became alert. Those members who usually showed up only on special Sundays, to cleanse their souls murmured, "This shit is going to be good, I'm glad I came."

Bishop Shackles then continued:

In addition, they are both heavy with children.

The congregation remained silent like the Church mouse. He then resumed his sermon:

Also, sitting here on my left is the first lady, Assistant Bishop, Mrs. Shackles, my other soul. On her left is Dr. Dansford, our music director, the lovely mother of Alice.

Don't y'all think they are beautiful and lovely?

Some member of the congregation responded with a warm and delayed applause while many sat in silence as they looked around to be sure they were in the right church, on Jesus' day of resurrection. Many were also wondering, what the heck is going on . . .

Over the past two or so years now, I have struggled with my own demons and demagogue. I prayed to the Lord to show me the right way. I prayed to Him to open my eyes, for I had been blinded to the challenges within my family and to some members in our flock. I especially prayed to Him to show me the right path to follow.

Last week, the Lord asked me to cleanse myself before him. That, I'll do in your presence today.

Let me quote some scriptures that would be the basis of my sermon today. Please, turn to Matthew 7:27-29

"Judge not, that you be not judged. For with the judgment you pronounce you will be judged, and with the measure you use, it will be measured to you. Why do you see the speck that is in your brother's eye, but do not notice the log that is in your own eye? Or how can you say to your brother, 'Let me take the speck out of your eye,' when there is the log in your own eye? You hypocrite, first take the log out of your own eye, and then you will see clearly to take the speck out of your brother's eye."

All my life, I have devoted myself to His words. All my life, I have walked in His ways according to his words. Like Abraham who was asked to sacrifice his son, my faith was tested with the sexual orientation and preference of my loving daughter, Samoa.

Until today, I had failed my Lord. Until now, I had failed all of you. Above all, I had failed my loving and caring daughter.

Today, I have removed the specks in my own eyes so that I can see with 20/20 vision and admit my sins.

Today, I want to tell my daughter in the presence of this congregation and the world, that I love her and forever will support her. She is part of me. She is a loving, hardworking, responsible, productive, respectful, and caring daughter. She's the sunshine of my life and the joy of our entire family. I can't ask God for a better daughter.

If my daughter had done what's abominable, then, she had violated the same sins committed by many we pray the Almighty God to forgive in our preaching and prayers every day, every night, every Sunday, and everywhere we saved souls—my soul and your souls.

I want all of you to stand up and hug the person on your right and the person on your left and say, my brother or sister or mother or father or uncle or nephew or niece or friends or stranger; I love you as Jesus Christ loved His children and the church. And when you get home today, I want you to hug the rest of your family who should have been in church with you today, and express your love to them as well. Then, go to your neighbors and say, I love you neighbor, regardless of their point of views, race or color. Break bread with them if you must . . .

Let me refer you to 1 Corinthians 6:9-10:

"Do you not know that the wicked will not inherit the kingdom of God? Do not be deceived: Neither the sexually immoral nor idolaters nor male prostitutes nor homosexual offenders nor thieves nor the greedy nor drunkards nor slanderers nor swindlers will inherit the kingdom of God."

I will come back to that later.

I have sinned by embracing, directly or indirectly, the same sins committed by God's children we pray for and forgive every day, for their inequities— children trafficking, sexual abuse, structural and despicable corruption, infant mortality, poverty, killings, and atrocities, too many to mention here.

Now, I ask you, my brethren, can we say with a clear conscience that homosexuality is a greater sin?

The homosexuals we condemned are our God's children. The homosexuals we hate are humans created by Him. The lesbians we condemned are children of many we profess to love, work for, and many we called our friends and heroes. They are our children. They are your sons. They are your daughters, my daughters, and our children's children.

Many of the homosexuals we despised and wanted to kill or cast aside are governors, senators, congressmen and women, movie stars, news casters, talk show hosts, preachers, corporate executives, business men and women, city mayors, truck drivers, construction workers, and teachers.

Many of them are the poor and the rich. They are your neighbors, your brothers, your mothers, your sisters, your cousins, your fathers, and many more, all over the world.

And yes, just as some of my brothers and sisters, sitting amongst us here today, they are doing great things for themselves and mankind.

Some we quick so condemn, absolutely, are men and women leaders around the world. Many we refused to recognize are adding values to the lives of others in need, as prescribed to us by the scriptures.

At the same time, we celebrate some of them as long as we ignored their true existence or we just don't want to know. Many of us accepted their gifts and donations directly and indirectly and turn blind eyes to the sins we officially condemned in exchange for the almighty currencies. It reminded of me our old military policy of "Don't ask, don't tell."

I heard or read about my people and your people from the Bible belt states, flocking into social swingers' clubs every weekend. I've seen my people, and your people, sending ungodly and indecent pictures to under-age same sex boys or girls.

And yet, many of the same people stood in the presence of the Lord each Sunday with their tailor-made garments and condemned, in public, the sins of others and their inequities.

Now, I ask all of you, what is more important, the sexual orientation of a person or his or her deeds?

My Lord is the King of love. My Lord is the King of peace. My Lord is the King of affection. I'll say it now and loudly that as for me and my house; we will henceforth serve Him the right way.

Today, I ask you to love others regardless of their color, gender, sexual orientation, and country of birth. If we do not, I am certain the day will come when enough of you will begin to hate everyone else just for the color of his or her blood type because it's not the color of your blood type. And in the end, you will begin to hate yourself, your family, and your neighbors since there is no one else to hate. I see such hatred coming, if not already here with us—mass killing of innocent children and adults are good examples. Children killing their parents and parents killing their children are common today than ever. Bombing innocent people at event gathering is another.

My brethren, we are already behind the eight ball on this single issue because many states of the union are legalizing same sex marriages. The supreme court of the land had added its neutral voice to the matter. Sooner than later, same sex marriages would become the law of the land, whether we support it or not. We are in a new world of social-democracy, and I don't see any end to its tentacles.

I've searched my soul, brothers and sisters, and know I have sinned. I know I'm created by the Almighty and heterosexual, and yet, I can't explain why I'm. I just know I'm.

By the same measure, my daughter is created by the Almighty God and a lesbian, and yet, she can't explain why she is a lesbian. She just knows she is.

My daughter just wanted to be loved. I'd failed to love and support that aspect of her life, thus far.

Today, I submit to you that my daughter hadn't sinned. And if she had sinned, she had been forgiven by our Lord Jesus Christ when He created her, died for her, just as He had created the rest of us, died for us, and forgave all our sins on the cross, at Golgotha.

Matthew 5:43-48 taught us this much:

You have heard that it was said; you shall love your neighbor and hate your enemy. But I say to you, love your enemies and pray for those who persecute you, so that you may be sons of your Father who is in heaven. For he makes his sun rise on the evil and on the good and sends rain on the just and on the unjust. For if you love those who love you, what reward do you have? Do not even the tax collectors do the same? And if you greet only your brothers, what more are you doing than others? Don't even the Gentiles do the same? You therefore must be perfect, as our heavenly Father is perfect.

In the world of today, burdened by poverty, illiteracy, slavery, religious prosecutions, sexual abuse, sexual discrimination, infant mortality, inadequate educational opportunities, senseless killings, terrorism, abuse of power, bad corruption, good corruption, diseases, and many other sinful acts, our profession, I beg your pardon, our churches and their leaders, isolate and discriminate against those who couldn't control their beings. Thus far, they have focused on one sin among many sins—homosexuality.

For I have sinned. Today, I want all of you to pray for me and my family. I will do the same as I have always done for all of you over the years.

Bishop Shackles wiped drops of tears from his cheeks and sipped a drink of water with lemon, to wet his lips. As he lifted up his head, nearly everyone could see that his eyes were red. He was perspiring, and the sun-rays were shinning upon him through the stained glass windows from the east. He seemed shaking from emotions and the burden of troubled world around him, but at peace. He turned around and faced the altar and prayed for the strength to continue his sermon. Everyone on the stage and some members of the congregation started wiping tears from their faces. His wife walked over to him, hugged him, and went back to her seat without altering a word. His daughter, Samoa, did the same. Alice and Samoa embraced and held hands.

As Bishop Shackles turned around to face the congregation one more time, he appeared possessed by the Holy Ghost. However, he looked refreshed, and energized. His white robe looked golden, and a few in the assemblage, are ready to give testimony because they swore they saw halo circling over his head. He continued his sermon, this time, with visible tears running down his cheeks, as his wife stood and walked over to stand beside him:

We have no right to discriminate against anyone as everyone discriminates against us, but we do. We have no right to be prejudiced against our fellowmen or women as many prejudiced against us, but we do.

We have no right to hate our neighbors, near or far, as many of our neighbors near and far continue to hate us, near and far, but we do. We have no right to advocate the killings of God's children as many of God's children continue to kill us for all reasons, but we do. We have no right to condemn others as many continue to condemn us, but we do. We have no right to ignore the powerless and the unfortunate people in our country and around the world, as many ignore the plights of many poor and powerless in our mist, and around the world, but we do.

Now I ask of you, are we different from those we condemned and cast aside, from many that condemned and cast us aside for any reasons?

We must learn to forgive even those we consider sinners by the scriptures or by our interpretations of His words.

Let me also remind you of the gospel according to Luke 20:46-47:

Beware of the scribes, who desire to go around in long robes, love greetings in the marketplaces, with the best seats in the synagogues, and the best places at feasts, which devour widows' houses, and for a pretense make long prayers. These will receive greater condemnation.

Yesterday, I had directed our churches in Africa to keep the house of the Lord open to all races, gender, sexual orientation, and religious persuasion. Our church must pray for all souls: men, women, young and old, rich and poor, the healthy, the sick, and the weak . . . We can no longer pick and choose which sins to condemn and which ones to embrace. This world is a stage. None of us will be on any stage forever.

Close your eyes for a second and ask yourself one simple question, "What would our Lord say to the multitude, from the mountain tops, or on the banks of Galilee, on these issues?" Search your souls and answer this question the way our Lord Jesus Christ, the Yahweh of our faith, had answered them through His preaching according to the gospels.

Today, I had celebrated true Easter as it was meant to be—preaching love, understanding, forgiveness, and peace to the world. Glory, Glory, be to Him, everlasting, and hallelujah. Amen.

This may be a surprise to my daughter, in a fortnight; I've agreed to officiate her wedding with her partner in this house of the Lord. Everyone in this congregation is invited. I hope all of you, if by the evidence of the love you showed me today, will join me and my family for this joyous occasion . . .

Suddenly, a long, devoted, and one of the original founding family members of the church, led by their mother, Deaconess Mama Grace Johnson, stood with her husband and their children, and walked out of the assemblage. Grace was speaking aloud, as her entire family walked to their 2009 German-made SUV, "Why can't they just go to Jerry Springer and get married. That's where their kind does it?" Unbeknownst to her, her own children disagreed with her resolve because her middle aged son, pretty Longentivity, has not disclosed his sexual orientation to his parents. One of the church members who overheard Mama Grace's rant, commented, "And she watched *Springer show?*

All of a sudden, Bishop Shackles stopped the sermon. He wiped tears from his eyes. He felt whole, complete from within, and at peace. He went over to his daughter, Samoa, gave her a hug, and said, "My love, you will always be my African queen." He them turned to her partner, Alice, and said, "With love, I welcome you to our family."

Everyone on the stage hugged and cried together. The rest of the congregation joined them.

The house of worship, led by Bishop Shackles will never be the same.

Before Bishop Shackles could go back to his seat, the chairman of the trustee board stood and said, "Bishop Shackles, the vote is unanimous, you're and will always be our leader in this church and everywhere our church goes to plant the seeds and safe souls. We are one, and you have 110% of our support."

The stage is now set for the overseers of the South-East and North-East Church committee in Hatu to render their opinion on the fate of one of their own: Bishop Samuel Shackles, DD.

"With prayers, all things are possible," Bishop Shackles said aside.

Copies of his sermon on CDs, for a small donation, will be on sale in ten days, on Amazon.com and in the church's bookstore.

CHAPTER 22

At the Easter dinner, the second main event of the day, every invitee was present. It was a full house. The sitting arrangement placed Precious and Oko next to each other. Mrs. Shackles directed lovely Precious to sit beside Oko.

Immediately, a determined Precious, got up and moved to another seat at the far end of the table with her daughter, Moji, clutched to her bosom.

Bishop Shackles had expected her reaction. He excused himself from the table, and quickly summoned his wife and Precious to his library for a fatherly honest-to-goodness talk with Precious. He had had enough of her drama, selfishness, and immaturity.

The Bishop looked directly into Precious' eyes, and said:

> *Precious, we love you and you ought to know that by now. We want the best for you and your family. This time, however, I am going to talk to you from the heart. I'm also going to cut out the psychology and counseling crap. I'll skip the mumbo jumbo as well and talk straight to you, the way a loving but stern father should talk to his daughter.*

> *Precious, you're going to get your behind right back to that table and sit as we arranged it, period. You're old enough to be considerate and rational. It's about time to stop your selfishness for a change. You need*

> *to cool down that overheated 'me only' brain of yours. By the way, let him see his daughter, Moji, and cut out the "Meet me in court," bull-shit.*

"Lord, please forgive my foul language," he said.

Florence concurred with him and said, "Amen to that Bishop."

He then continued:

> *I'll remind you of an African proverb, "Who forgives win." It's time to forgive him for whatever he did.*
>
> *My wife almost divorced me because of you. It was the power of prayers and the blessing of God Almighty that kept us together.*
>
> *So, grow up and do what is right for once in your life. You have a nice man sitting out there who loves you more than himself. You have a beautiful daughter together, which by the way was a blessing and a miracle from God. Stop running and start thinking. Enough is enough. And by the way, you're not getting any younger.*
>
> *Oko loves you. He even refused to take you to court so that he could see his daughter. Look in the mirror Dr. Dansford, and see beyond your pretty face . . .*
>
> *Now, get your butt back to the dinner table and let's enjoy the Easter dinner my wife make especially for both of you. We will always love you . . .*

Bishop Shackles walked back to the dining table. Precious almost fainted as she stood up and followed in tow. She went back to sit beside Oko. Oko was a gentleman. He stood up for her to sit beside him, and smiled as if he has just won the lottery. "Thanks Mr. Oko," she said and gave Moji, their daughter, to him for the first time in the presence of the multitude.

Moji knew she was with her father. Everyone in the room felt it as well. They saw the way the little girl laid on her father's chest and was trying to say, "Daaada." Oko, for the first time presented Moji to everyone and said, "This is our daughter, Ife. Her name means love."

Precious then remembered 1 Kings 3:27

> *Then the king answered and said, Give her the living child, and in no wise slay it: she is the mother thereof.*

Moji finally belongs to her father, Oko. Many in the mist, including Alice and Samoa, didn't even know Oko had been working overtime with Precious. All Alice, her daughter could do was opened her mouth in surprise, looked around the room, and said, "Excuse you?"

It was time for dinner prayers and Oko was asked to do the honor of rendering the invocation. Like a minister wants-to-be, he delivered the best dinner prayer everyone had ever heard. It lasted fifteen minutes. Some guests were silently drinking their ice tea and munching on their cornbread during his prayer . . .

He would be a dynamic preacher one day, Precious said to herself. Her dream of being a pastor's wife one more time may probably come to pass.

Oko prayed for love, forgiveness, and in a unique way, he thanked everyone present by name. He particularly thanked Bishop Shackles and his wife, Mrs. Florence Shackles. He asked for their forgiveness because he had sinned against them.

But they'd forgiven him even before he asked. Bishop Shackles and his household were truly the agents of God in a rare form.

Before dinner, Bishop Shackles asked his guests at the table to introduce themselves.

Present were:

Bishop Shackles, Mrs. Shackles, their daughter Samoa and her two brothers; Alice and her sons: Al and Sam. Precious and her younger daughter, Moji, Oko and his other three children, Dr. Diick—the father of Alice's children, and ten other invited guests, including the mother of the local news anchor, Sunni, who is also the godmother to Bishop Shackles' boys.

Certainly, the news of the Easter dinner will be on the eleven o'clock news, on BPTV, channel 12 at 11.

In the background playing softly was *Family Affair* by Mary J. Blige.

The food was delicious and everyone present was pleased as they each thanked their hosts for the dinner. They gave glory to the Almighty God for the feast and the soil that produced them. They also prayed for millions that may go hungry this night across America and the rest of the world, the same way they had prayed for hundred years . . .

Frankly, the dinner would have been more suited for Thanksgiving instead.

Towards the end of the dinner, Oko stood and asked Bishop Shackles for permission to speak.

"Brother Oko, this is your house, you can talk here anytime without permission," Bishop Shackles replied. Everyone in attendance shook their heads and concurred, by saying aloud, "That's right."

Oko cleared his throat and thanked his sister, assistant Bishop Florence Shackles, for her support and love once again. He thanked Bishop Shackles for his fatherly and pastoral guidance for him, his family, the church, and his constant generous affections to everyone, and everywhere.

"Bishop Shackles was truly the keeper of the Lord's flock," he said.

He then turned to Precious and knelt down in front of her and said,

"Prie, I want to thank you in particular for your love, affection, and devotion to our daughter, Ife. You are a great mother. I know things haven't been as we had planned. I realized I made wrong turns along the way during the beginning of our relationship but I want to tell you in front of our entire loving family and friends here today that I love you. I'll always be in love with you just as I did the first day I laid eyes on you at the mission-community chicken dinner sale that warm Saturday afternoon. Let's start a new beginning. Let's open a new page in our memory book, for the rest of our lives."

He then reached into his pocket and brought out a four carat diamond engagement ring and said, "My love, would you give me my happiness and peace back, and be my wife?

It's not necessary to dwell on the sources of his wealth to justify the expensive diamond at this happy occasion. Frankly, no one cared. The size of the ring was everybody's focal point.

Everyone in the room was dead silent. All present could hear an ant piss on cotton. They were eager and waiting for Precious to respond. Mrs. Shackles shifted in her seat, looked directly at Precious, as if anxious for a positive answer. Even Bishop Shackles was on edge and silently praying . . .

Precious was under pressure. She had been ambushed. She saw it coming since the dinner invitation but had ignored her suspicion.

She asked Oko Yembe to get off his knees. The air seemed to be at a standstill, and those of little faith, sitting at the table, were predicting a rejection, or at least, a delayed acceptance.

A handful of the guests must be saying amongst themselves, "Look at this fool. He should just shorten his misery and run as far as he could from here." One of the Pharisees, with a hat as if going on a safari, turned to the person sitting next to her and said, "Darn, I hope he had a kneel pad, otherwise, he better put on his Kenyan's marathon pair of legs, track shoes, and run as fast as he could." Oko wasn't even a Kenyan born. It seems all Africans look alike.

"No, he probably needs the legs of Usain Bolt of Jamaica," said a local radio, middle aged weather reporter, who had been engaged six times to four different men and one woman within the last five years.

Precious thanked everyone present, especially Bishop Shackles for his fatherly love and direction in her life. She then went over to Mrs. Shackles and gave her a hug. She started sniffing and Oko offered her a tissue. Some dinner guests stopped chewing their food as they waited anxiously for her to get to the main point. The chairman of the deacon board, Professor Johnson J. Johnson, refreshed his wine glass and held his wife's hand. He was once more than just a friend to Precious, his former graduate student. His wife knew about the affairs but held on to her man. Smart lady . . .

Precious smiled and waved to her daughter, Alice, and her partner, Samoa.

She then went back to Oko, held his hands, kissed him passionately for the first time in public, and knelt down in front of him.

Quoting Barbara Rush in the 1959 movie, *The Young Philadelphians*, she said, "I'm an institution now." After a pulse, she then said, "Are you sure, you still want to marry me?"

Without hesitation, Oko emphatically replied, "Yes my love, it would be a blessing and a dream comes true to marry you, if you would've me."

"Ok then, my love, I'll marry you for the rest of my life," she responded.

Unrehearsed, everybody in the room shouted, "Halleluiah, thank you Jesus." Some started singing the church's favorite song, *bless this love, oh Lord. Bless your children as they have accepted you as their father because you are our only father on earth and in heaven . . .*

The best champagne in the house was served for the celebration of another family love affairs united. The entire house of Bishop Shackles and guests got on their feet with the loudest applause. They hugged for what seemed to last forever. They sang and prayed individually for Oko and Precious as if they were in a chanting festival from the horn of Africa.

The middle aged local radio celebrity immediately opened her purse and poured some sort of brown liquid from a pink stainless, pocket size flask, into her tea cup.

Unbeknownst to her, Bishop Shackle was watching her in action at a distance. She was embarrassed when she realized that the Bishop saw her. She felt guilty of the sin she just committed in the presence of a holy man. To her surprise, Bishop Shackle went over to her and said, "Sister Karolyn, top my tea cup too, please." Definitely, when Jesus Christ turned water into wine, He did it for all His children, Bishop Shackle and the weather girl included.

Thereafter, the real merriment began . . .

Precious, after the applause subsided, announced, "Y'all, we just got engaged folk and our wedding day has been set 30 days from today." The applause resumed. Alice and Samoa hugged and kissed tenderly.

The single females or those loosely attached to anybody, were now crying because they hadn't found their own Oko, to-date.

The mother of the local TV personality asked aloud, "Why the hurry?"

Precious replied, "I want the barracudas to know my love is branded and off limit."

Everybody shakes their heads and said, "That's right girl, hold on to your man from those hungry cats . . . ."

Any new arrivals to the dinner would have thought the President of the United States of America was delivering the State of the Union Address with all the intermittent applauses from members of congress. This time, however, everyone in the room was applauding together as one family, for the love of one family, in a one party household, among people of like minds, indivisible by the powers of the Almighty.

Finally, the family love affairs had come in full circle: Alice, Samoa, Precious, and Oko. Bishop Shackles then blessed the future Mr. and Mrs. Oko and read from Deuteronomy 28:8

> *The Lord shall command the blessing upon thee in*
> *thy storehouses, and in all that thou sets thine hand*
> *unto; and He shall bless thee in the land which the*
> *Lord thy God given thee.*

Within ten minutes, Mrs. Shackles, on behalf of her family and church, offered to be responsible for the wedding arrangements and expenditures. She was always like that. She loves her family. She loves her brother, Oko . . .

Bishop Shackles checked his calendar and said, "Guess what folk, I'm wide open and the church is available thirty days from today to perform the wedding." He went on to make another announcement, "I'm also happy to announce that, the trustee board, wants me to inform y'all that they had approved Brother Oko as an Associate Preacher (AP), effective immediately. Congratulations, Preacher Oko."

Another long applause and hugging followed. Oko was short of words. He could only stand, nod his head, and say, "Thank you." Precious was elated and a little closer to her dreams . . .

When the merriment was almost over, Mrs. Shackles volunteered to babysit Moji and Oko's other children so that the newly engaged couple could celebrate alone. Oko anxiously wanted to share intimate love in earnest with Precious. She needed and wanted him too.

Celebrate they intend to do. Anyone with sensitive buds in the room would've smelled Precious wet pussy aroma. Oko's dick was at ninety degrees so much so that he couldn't stand up to face the guests until Precious stood in front of him to cover his erection. She kissed him as they both turned around and exited the room.

As it turned out, she had always wanted him more than he knew. These were the facts summarized from her diary, page 453 to 497:

Precious had registered for at least two additional graduate courses with him after she had satisfied her graduation requirements just to keep a close eye on him.

She once lied to some of her friends whom she thought might be interested in him by saying, "Y'all better leave him alone. The son-of-a-bitch is probably married to ten wives in the jungle of Africa."

They all laughed and thereafter thought of him in their wet dreams.

She had forever marked her territory from the rest of the vultures—she probably described them as bunch of wolves . . .

"I saw him first and y'all losers can have my left over," she always said to herself.

She gambled on Oko and won.

Most importantly, she had waited several times to watch Oko walked away as she admired his butt. To her, that was his sexiest part. In a sense, she was a butt-lady. Riodiaz, her ex, had her type of butt but Oko had her perfect butt. Many nights, she wished she could hold them, squeeze them, and ride him senselessly while holding his butt. Her thought of his butt turned her on. The sight of his butt made her wet and gave her goose bumps. The only thing left for her until the real butt came to her was to dream of the man with the golden African butt.

If she had known he was Florence's brother when she first saw him, she would have wanted to fuck him just one time and dumped him thereafter. The thought of him made her come alive. The sight of him made her nipples hard. The memories of him had made her changed her panties, trice a day, countless days. One of those days was the day he brought flowers to her office.

During her disastrous church wedding that never was with her former fiancé, Jeremy, she had hoped Oko would rescue her like a white knight. She had wished he would take her away into the horizon, and fuck her the way he did the evening Moji was conceived in his apartment, during her Banku dinner. She remembered the day, like today . . . In her soul, she knew true love exists at the right time, on her watch with Oko.

Oko drove her to her home which was less than fifteen miles away. They hardly got into the door before all pieces of their attire went everywhere. By the time they got to her bed, she was stark naked, and was breathing heavily as if she had been running away from a hungry Lion. Her breathing was sexual and erotic. She was ready to make up for the lost steaming and passionate sex with him since their tour of America . . . .

On the other hand, Oko wanted to unload his cargo he had been carrying within his "Long John."

But first, she turned on her smart phone and replayed a poem by Onyinye V. Obioha.

She had recorded it in her own voice. Listening to her sexy voice on tape with the erotic poem made Oko's temperature rose above normal. He couldn't take it anymore. He wanted to make love to his love and fiancée. Her voice had become an aphrodisiac. She set the smart phone on repeat.

He knew it was going to be a long night. She was equally ready with every hole in her body. The room was dark. She turned on only the hallway light and pulled up the window blinds. She wasn't thinking about the neighbors this time around. After all, her man is in the house . . .

Her voice came alive:

> *Tonight he whispered in my ears*
> *I could hear the crickets chirping noisily*
> *Anticipating the rhythm of the night*
> *Tracing the moonlight curves*
>
> *He lay me down in the meadow*
> *Soaking my heart with a pool of desire*
> *The stars begin to twinkle as each caress bring me*
> *closer to the horizon with a swift embrace, I became*
> *lost in the wind*
>
> *Together we dined and wined*
> *Pulsating with each movement of the clouds*
> *Filling the night with more wine*
> *Gingerly we soared like an eagle*
> *Sated in the fountain of desire*
> *We reveled in the chanting of the night*
>
> *Lost in the abyss, we lost our sanity*
> *Mocked by the hills and valleys*
> *Shamelessly displaying the untamed souls*
> *In our stupor we discovered another new rhythm*
> *Flowing with the melody of the east wind baring the*
> *night of its darkness*

Dance, we danced
Ride, we rode all night
Till we emptied this vessel of yearning
Of love and lust
Of desire and passion
Of want and need
Oh dawn, why break so early
Knowing the night will never cease to hide in the
*   shadows of our memory*

Their love making was like the first time. It was definitely better than the second. The bed sheet was dripping with hot sweat. The pillow cases were wet. She could hardly regain her breath before Oko started to ride her as if he was running a one hundred dash. If their past was any guide, Moji 2 may be baking nicely in the oven. This time, however, he was praying for a boy . . . African men will always be Africans to the core: all children are celebrated at birth but boys are especially celebrated. Every African man knows it, every African woman agrees . . .

Precious couldn't breathe. She wanted to come up for air. She was sweating profusely. Her body was wet and slippery. Her pussy was erupting lava juice and slippery. He was doing his best to keep his dick in her slippery pussy. He turned on the air conditioner with the bedside remote control. The temperature outside was 51 degrees. The glass windows were frosty and sweating . . .

Too bad, poor Rodney, the boy with the golden binoculars, who had in the past been watching Precious nude, in the rain, had moved away from the neighborhood. He would have had his eyes full as Oko and Precious were perfecting their animal magnetism for all to see through her wide open windows, without curtains.

Any busy-body or trespassers, walking by her windows, would have heard Oko and Precious going at it. With that knowledge, she wouldn't give a shit. She had always been her neighbors' favorite American, especially to all men and some women of all color, race, and shape—true neighborhood perverted rainbow souls.

Oko held her and led her into the shower. They needed a break and recharge their batteries. He lathered and bathed her like a delicate two-year old baby. They washed each other's back. He massaged her breasts and pussy as if he were a specialist in human anatomy. They bathed each other again and again and talked about their first date, for the most part. They walked into the Jacuzzi and spent time talking about nothing . . . Her pussy was sore. They were kissing and practically eating each other's body parts like a calf sucking her mother's breasts. She sat on his dick as the water jets, at full speed, massaged their private parts clinched together. Oko was quickly learning the American ways about women, sex, and sexuality.

He whispered, "Prie, how am I doing?"

"Hush, don't stop my love," she said with a voice hardly audible.

He asked her to turn around so that he could make love to her from behind. Her only request was, "Could I please, put a lubricant at the tip of my clit and a little virgin oil on your dick before you stick me?"

"Why honey?" he asked. Poor Oko, he still has a lot to know and assimilate in the new land and women sojourned therein.

"Please, I need to cool down your pussy . . . if you don't know, your giant chocolate dick almost tore me into pieces . . . ," she was almost begging.

Precious, for the first time in her life, got all she asked for and more in a man. The man is Oko.

"O, please, do me on the couch, I want my own memory," she demanded, as she recollected their first time on his couch, in his apartment. That stain looks like the map of Lake Victoria.

As if he was on a mission to throw a shot-put in the Olympic, he gently lifted her up with his strong arms and walked towards the couch as if carrying a bouquet of flowers to Miss America on stage. He slowly laid her on her couch like an endangered flower. Slowly, he meticulously licked around her labia and rested finally on her wet pussy. It was his second time to do so. She knew his performance have improved, even though not as perfect as she would have liked. He was practically worshipping her clit as if the angels were in the house judging his performances in other to earn his wings. Oko's current performance was not what she wanted for the rest of the night . . . She knew she would teach him the right way to eat her pussy in due time. For now, she wanted him to handle his perfect act perfectly.

She lifted his head and pushed his lips towards her lips, kissed him to have a taste of her own blessed wetness, and then directed him to do what he does best—fuck her mercilessly . . . left, right, front, circle, and center.

She then placed her hands behind her butt, lifted them up, and spread her legs extra wide to take-in his entire endowed instrument. "This is my joyous night of okoism," she was telling herself as she priced herself lucky to have him at last to herself exclusively, in peace, and without guilt.

Oko started pumping her pussy recklessly. He was greedy and selfish without apology. "She is all mine now and I can do her, as I like it, as she likes it, when she likes it, and when I like it," he murmured. Finally, every ounce of juicy Precious belongs to him.

"Honey, take it easy, my pussy is on fire . . . give me a break, please. We have a lifetime to catch up," she incoherently pleaded, for the second time. She had met all she ever dreamt in any man. She loved every inch of him.

He started sucking her hard nipples. Even though she had stopped nursing her daughter months ago, her nipples still produced traces of fresh sugar free, and vitamin A-Z breast milk. The poor innocent little child had just shared her mother's milk, with her own father, with the same tits, that used to belong to her exclusively, for the past seventeen months.

Oko was about to get up for a drink of water when Precious held him down, and said, "Babe, where do you think you going?" "Honey, I thought you want a break?"

"Heck no, fuck me silly . . . I'm going to get mine for all the months I had deprived myself of you. You starved me since I stayed away from you. Get the ice, you will need it. You're going to make love to me all night, even if it kills me."

As he got up for a drink of water and the ice, he looked at the clock. It was 4:14 am.

"Honey, do you know how long we've been at this?"

"Are you complaining, dear?" "Not at all, not at all, my love."

Exhausted, they fell asleep from joy and satisfaction. They were peaceful for the first time in months. At that instant, their past pains from all sources evaporated—they were now sailing peacefully under God's speed. Heavens, 555 Love Lane, OldPort, is the best place on earth . . .

Update:

An elaborate month-long African traditional wedding in the presence of Oko's family and his entire Kurumbe village, in 90 days, is planned for two weeks. An ex-President of a West African country, who is now the king of his village, uncle Dudu's cousin, and also Oko's former mentor at the ministry, will be the special guest of honor.

According to their Facebook pages and twitter postings, the whole world is invited.